# A loud bang vibrated through the plane.

The Beech swerved and shuddered from the impact of the explosion in the right-wing engine, and a sudden show of saw-toothed flames raced along the wing.

"We're going down! Brace yourselves!" the pilot cried, sweat flowing down his face as he tried to raise the plane's nose.

"*¡Cristo!*" Encizo rasped in answer to Manning's muffled oath. There wasn't anything they could do as the Beech whirled and cut a crazy pattern in the frigid air. The angry buzz saw of the remaining engine screamed in their ears, and their vision became a wild blur as the frozen ground approached, threatening to crumple the plane into a great metal fist.

## Mack Bolan's
# PHOENIX FORCE®

# PHOENIX FORCE.

# Power Gambit

## Gar Wilson

A GOLD EAGLE BOOK FROM
**WORLDWIDE.**

TORONTO · NEW YORK · LONDON · PARIS
AMSTERDAM · STOCKHOLM · HAMBURG
ATHENS · MILAN · TOKYO · SYDNEY

First edition March 1988

ISBN 0-373-61334-2

Special thanks and acknowledgment to
William Fieldhouse for his contribution to this work.

Printed in Canada

## 1

The cold wind howled like a monstrous beast from the dark regions of a terrible nightmare. Edward Hamilton prayed that it was just part of a bad dream. He prayed he would awake to find himself safe in the apartment back in Helsinki, even if his pajamas were soaked with sweat and his wife was upset with him for thrashing around in bed. But he didn't care about all that, just as long as he woke up.

But the nightmare seemed to last forever, and Hamilton realized he wouldn't escape it by opening his eyes. He was not dreaming the nightmare. He was living it.

Edward and Marsha Hamilton had been visiting Kemijai when the nightmare began. They were supposed to meet with the governor of the province of Lappi. It was a social engagement, informal diplomacy to express the good will of the United States embassy to the people of northern Finland.

The role of the American diplomatic corps was hardly considered critical in Finland. The Scandinavian nation's parliamentary democracy maintained friendly relations with the United States and other countries of the free world. The government of Finland is stable, and the economy strong, despite occasional bouts with inflation. The people of Finland enjoy a high standard of living, have good education and engage in prosperous trade with numerous countries throughout the world.

Of special interest to the United States is the fact that the Soviet Union is one of Finland's next-door neighbors. The Communist superpower is located at the eastern border of Finland, and that hardy nation follows a path of neutrality to avoid conflict with the USSR. But neutrality doesn't mean immunity from power politics and intrigue in international affairs.

Edward Hamilton was the chief aide to the U.S. ambassador. That was a rather obscure title, and Hamilton's duties tended to be equally vague. He had been grateful to be sent to Lappi, because it helped justify his job. Every time Washington started to talk about trimming the fat off the bureaucracy, Hamilton worried that he would be among the federal government employees to get the ax.

He wished he had been fired. He wished he had wound up on the unemployment line instead of being in the fearful situation he and his wife were faced with.

The nightmare had begun when the embassy limousine was approaching Kemijai. The car made slow progress due to weather conditions. Traffic jams aren't much of a problem in Finland, especially in the northern province of Lappi. More than two-thirds of the entire population live in the southern portions of the country. But the slick, icy roads and carpets of dense snow made travel difficult, if not dangerous.

The driver was familiar with the roads and experienced in handling such formidable driving conditions. He had assured the Hamiltons that he had driven in nasty weather every winter since he was sixteen. The driver was from Michigan. He was as good as his word and drove along the treacherous road with admirable skill. The limo skidded several times on the ice, but the driver moved with it and steered the car back on track with little effort. Of course he drove slowly. It was better to take their time getting to Kemijai than to wind up buried in a snowdrift along the side of the road.

They encountered the roadblock roughly twenty miles from their destination. Two large trucks extended lengthwise across the road, and three men in olive-drab parkas moved between the vehicles. Hamilton would have been suspicious of the roadblock if the limo had been traveling through Italy, Greece or France. But Finland wasn't plagued by terrorist activity or militant extremists. A snow-covered road in Lappi seemed the most unlikely place in the world for an ambush.

The driver stopped the limo and got out of the car to see what the problem was. He was no more worried than his employer. Finland was hardly Lebanon or Northern Ireland. He approached the trucks calmly and called out a greeting in Finnish, then summoned up one-tenth of his entire Finnish vocabulary.

"Yes," one of the men replied as he stepped forward, "I do speak English. Little bit, eh? You American?"

"Yeah," the driver answered. He noticed something odd about the man's accent. The guy didn't sound like a Finn speaking English, but the driver couldn't figure out what the accent suggested. "Yes. We're Americans. What's the problem here?"

"Problem?" the spokesman of the group began with a smile. "We have no problem."

He reached inside a pocket of his parka and drew a blue-black pistol. The driver's mouth fell open in astonishment and fear as the gun barrel canted upward. The stranger calmly squeezed the trigger. The pistol snarled, and a lead projectile with a steel core tore into the roof of the driver's open mouth. The bullet expanded when it struck bone. Lead split the upper jawbone while the steel core sliced into the driver's brain.

"Now," the gunman remarked, still smiling, "you don't have any problems, either."

The other two men by the trucks immediately rushed to the limo. They pulled compact machine pistols from inside their coats, deadly close-range weapons with stubby barrels. Edward and Marsha Hamilton sat in the back seat, spellbound by the abrupt shock of witnessing the unexpected murder of the embassy chauffeur. They sat as motionless and frozen as the icy ground surrounding the car.

Hamilton stared through the windows at the advancing gunmen. They resembled each other. Both men were large and muscular, although their thick parkas might have contributed to the impression of their formidable size. They had blue eyes, Nordic features and beards trimmed roughly in the same style. One man's beard was red and the other's was blond, but the hardness of their eyes and tightly shut lips seemed identical. To Hamilton, the gunmen appeared to be evil clones produced by a satanic wizard.

The ambassador's aide tried not to look at the black muzzles of the weapons pointed at the windows—

pointed at Edward and Marsha Hamilton. He didn't know much about firearms, but he realized the guns were automatic weapons of some sort. He sat helpless, pinned to the back seat of the limo by the threat of the evil twins and their blasters. Hamilton trembled with fear and shame. He had sat useless and terrified as he and Marsha had watched the first gunman kill the driver.

God, Hamilton thought with embarrassment, he didn't even know the chauffeur's name. Of course, the man had been introduced to him, but he had forgotten the driver's name two minutes after he'd heard it. It hadn't seemed important at the time. Hamilton felt he should have known the poor bastard's name. A man shouldn't die anonymously.

Hamilton was ashamed because he had taken no action when the killing had occurred. He hadn't known what to do, and he probably would have been too scared to take action even if he had known. Worse yet, he was unable to protect his wife. Poor Marsha had always relied on him to look after her, to see to her needs and desires. Now he had been humiliated before her eyes. The sons of bitches had reduced him to a trembling, fear-frozen statue, and he couldn't do a damn thing to protect himself or his beloved spouse.

The harsh report of another gunshot startled Hamilton. Marsha cried out with fear and closed her eyes tightly, as if trying to blot out the assassins by simply refusing to look at them. Edward Hamilton realized the shot had come from the first killer's pistol. The murderer had fired another bullet into the back of the driver's skull.

"No such thing as killing an enemy too dead, eh?" the gunman announced as he stepped toward the limo. "You two get out of car, please. Olav and Larrs won't hesitate to shoot if you don't do exactly what I tell you to. You understand this? My English may be not so good, but I think you understand gun, eh?"

The Hamiltons were too frightened to move.

"I tell you polite to get out of car," the man in charge of the ambush said with a sigh. "You stay in car, and I tell Olav and Larrs to shoot you both. Okay with me. You want this?"

Edward and Marsh Hamilton slowly emerged from the limousine. The bearded henchmen closed in. They shoved the American couple against the side of the car and roughly pulled back their arms to snap handcuffs on their wrists. The gunmen made certain the prisoners' wrists were locked at the small of their backs.

"Cooperation," the leader of the trio remarked as he approached. "I am glad you decide to cooperate. This will make things easier for all of us, eh?"

The man removed a metal cigarette case from his parka and opened it to extract a black cigarette. He stuck it into his mouth and fired the end with a gold-plated lighter, then smiled at Edward and Marsha Hamilton as smoke drifted from his lips to be scattered by the wind.

The leader didn't look like a Finn, Hamilton thought, staring at the flat, cold features of their captor. The man's eyes were dark, and bangs of black hair extended from the hood of his parka to his brow. His eyes had an oriental cast. The man appeared to be Eurasian, possibly Mongol. Russian? Hamilton wondered as he tried to work some saliva into his dry mouth so he could speak.

"Who are you?" Hamilton demanded. "What do you want?"

"Who am I?" The ringleader cocked his head sideways and smiled at Hamilton. "I do not see why I should not tell you. I am Anatoliy Mikhailovich Kharkov. A pleasure to meet you, Mr. Hamilton, although I do not think you share this opinion, eh?"

"You're Russian?" Hamilton said stiffly. "KGB?"

"Very good, Mr. Hamilton," Kharkov confirmed with a nod. "I am with department known as Morkrie Dela—'Wet Work,' I think you call it in English, eh? You've heard of it?"

"No," Hamilton replied. "I'm a diplomat, not a spy for the CIA. I think you've made a terrible mistake."

"Is not mistake, Mr. Hamilton," Kharkov assured him. "You're to be sacrificed for the sake of my mission. Oh, I could tell you I am much sorry this has happened, but that is not truth of how I feel. I was selected for Morkrie Dela because Soviet state psychoanalysts think I have right personality for 'Wet Work.' Is *blood* wet. Understand?"

"You're an assassin?" Hamilton glared at Kharkov.

"So you do understand." The Russian smiled and nodded. "Soviet state psychoanalysts very smart. They make good choice with me because I like my work. People usually no good at things they do not like, eh?"

"You're going to kill us?" Marsha demanded, staring at the Russian in disbelief. "No! You can't!"

The thug with the red beard seized the woman from behind and adroitly stuck a knotted white cloth into her mouth. He secured the gag and tied the ends at the back of her head. Hamilton turned toward his wife's assailant, thinking that he had to help her or at least try. He couldn't stand by and watch them manhandle his wife without showing her that he had enough manhood to try to stop them.

Hamilton stepped toward the red-haired goon and prepared to throw a kick at the bastard. The blond clone suddenly grabbed the back of Hamilton's collar and stamped a boot into the back of his knee. Hamilton's leg buckled, and he fell to his knees. A gag was stuffed into his mouth and tied in place to silence him.

"Do not do anything stupid," Kharkov warned as he finished smoking his cigarette and fieldstripped the butt to get rid of the burning ash and pocket the remaining paper and tobacco. The cigarettes were Russian, and he didn't intend to leave the evidence in the snow. "There is nothing you can do except make this harder for yourselves. I am professional. You die very quick with little pain, unless you make trouble for me. Then you die slow and with more pain than you think possible. Choose either way. Makes no difference to me."

Hamilton was hauled to the nearest truck by the blond henchman, who was bigger, stronger and several years younger than Hamilton. Even if he hadn't been handcuffed, the American diplomat would have been powerless against the man. The ambushers simply wanted to make the task as easy as possible.

Marsha struggled in the grasp of the red-haired thug. Her efforts were hopeless, but at least she tried to resist being herded into the truck. Marsha kicked her opponent in the shin. He grunted and rammed a short punch into her narrow waist. The woman doubled up with a muffled groan, and the redhead grabbed the chain joining the cuffs at the small of her back to pull Marsha to the rear of the vehicle.

Edward Hamilton was outraged. He started to charge toward the redhead, but the blond henchman quickly drove a gloved fist into Hamilton's kidney. The American's body jerked from the pain, and the thug hit him again between the shoulder blades. Hamilton started to topple forward, but Kharkov and the blond man grabbed him, lifting the diplomat's feet off the ground.

"Is bad beginning," the Russian warned. He turned to the blond man. *"Nyet, Larrs."*

Larrs nodded in reply and helped Kharkov toss Hamilton unceremoniously into the back of the truck. The diplomat tumbled across the floorboards. He moaned through his gag as his shoulder popped loose at the joint. Marsha was curled up in a corner of the truck interior, her body racked by silent, repressed sobs.

"Olav," the Russian called to the red-haired henchman as he tossed him the keys to the truck. Olav snatched the keys in midair and nodded, then headed for the cab of the truck.

Kharkov and Larrs climbed into the back with Hamilton and Marsha. The Russian kept his pistol aimed at the couple while Larrs closed the tailgate and pulled a canvas tarp over the opening. Facing the prisoners, the captors sat on the floorboards while

Olav started the engine. The truck moved forward and rolled around the second vehicle.

"Sit quietly and enjoy the ride," Kharkov announced. His smile was visible despite the shadows within the truck. "It really won't be so bad. I'm a perfectionist. That is the right word for one who tries to do a job with perfection, eh? I kill very well. Quick and professional. You're really rather lucky, you know."

Marsha trembled fearfully, her face streaked with tears. Edward Hamilton felt totally helpless. His dislocated shoulder throbbed with pain as he sat on the cold floor of the truck, unable to take any action or even attempt to talk. He was a man of words, not physical action. Perhaps he could reason with Kharkov if he could work the gag loose.

But Hamilton realized that was a false hope. Kharkov was clearly an amoral sociopath of some sort. The homicidal maniac wouldn't listen to reason. Besides, Kharkov was a Soviet agent carrying out orders from the KGB. Why the hell had the KGB sent this grinning madman to murder him and his wife? Hamilton found himself wondering despite his pain and shock. Sure, the CIA and the NSA had agents operating from the American embassy. Virtually all foreign embassies slip in a few espionage agents from time to time. The KGB must have mistakenly decided he was a goddamn spy, Hamilton concluded.

How could a mistake like that happen? Well, the CIA had made more than its share of screwups in the past, Hamilton thought. No reason to believe the KGB would be more infallible than its American counterpart. Still, Hamilton couldn't understand how anyone could mistake him for a spy. It seemed utterly absurd. Surely even the KGB wouldn't want to murder innocent bystanders. Still, Kharkov had killed the embassy driver as calmly as one might stomp on a cockroach, and he apparently planned to murder Marsha, as well....

Suddenly Hamilton had a thought that gave him a glimmer of hope. Maybe the bastards kidnapped his wife in order to threaten her life to try to get Hamilton to spill his guts about whatever information they wanted to get out of him. Hell, it was even possible they were not really Communist agents. Maybe the guns were loaded with blanks. Maybe the driver hadn't really been killed and the whole damn thing was staged. Maybe they were working for the CIA or some other intel outfit that was trying to test Hamilton's loyalty.

He tried to convince himself that this theory was true, or at least that it might be true. But deep down, Hamilton didn't believe it. Kharkov was taking them somewhere to kill them. The Russian didn't seem to want any information. He simply wanted to kill them. Why had the Hamiltons been chosen to die? Why had Kharkov decided to take them from the roadside where the limo had been stopped? He could have executed them on the spot, just the way he had killed the embassy driver. What the hell was he up to?

"You're actually quite lucky that I'm handling this job," Kharkov continued, discussing assassination as calmly as though he were conversing about the weather. "I've met some sadists who enjoy inflicting pain on their subjects. I, however, take great pride in the fact my kills are quick and clean. We all must die, my friends. Ever see someone die from cancer or some other long-term illness? I'd rather die quickly from a bullet. Considering the nature of my profession, there is a very good chance I'll get my wish, eh?''

Kharkov chuckled at his own joke and took another black cigarette from his case. Pungent smoke filled the enclosed area as the truck continued to travel on to a destination unknown to Edward and Marsha Hamilton.

Hamilton avoided looking at his wife. He didn't want to see her eyes. He felt certain she would stare at him with hatred and accusation in her expression. His position with the federal government had put them both in danger, and he had been unable to protect her from the mysterious kidnappers. Hamilton wouldn't have blamed Marsha if she had despised him for failing her in this deadly crisis. He despised himself, although he had no idea what he could have done to avoid the situation, besides never joining the diplomatic corps to begin with. God, he had been assigned to Finland. Who would have expected something like this to happen here?

The ride seemed to last an eternity. Hamilton wondered if Kharkov intended to smuggle them across the border into the Soviet Union. The idea seemed absurd, but everything about the incident was insane. If the lunatics tried to sneak into the USSR, the Finnish border patrol might nail them. Hamilton tried to convince himself that that possibility presented a thin ray of hope, but he realized there was little chance of rescue.

Kharkov chatted with Larrs in fluent Finnish. Hamilton understood only a few words, and the conversation was virtually meaningless to him. He noticed that the men didn't look at each other as they spoke. Their attention remained locked on the two captives. At last the truck came to a halt. The American couple stiffened with fear, aware of what the end of the journey meant.

"I believe we've arrived," Kharkov announced. He peeled back the tarp and peered outside. "Yes. Olav has found a perfect spot for us."

The Russian pushed aside the tarp. The red-haired Olav had already left the cab of the truck and moved to the rear of the vehicle. He opened the tailgate and climbed into the back of the rig. A gust of snowy wind accompanied the henchman. Both Olav and Larrs moved toward the Americans.

"Don't cause any trouble for us," Kharkov warned, tapping the gloved palm of one hand with the barrel of his pistol. "It will not help you, and will only make this more unpleasant for you than it already is."

Hamilton tried to get up, but the lack of circulation in his legs robbed them of strength. Needles of pain lanced his numb limbs as he put his weight on his feet and tried to think of some way to fight back. He couldn't even attempt to kick Larrs or Olav because his legs refused to respond to his brain.

The blond Larrs seized the diplomat and hauled him to the opening. Olav handled Marsha in the same abrupt manner. Kharkov had already stepped down from the vehicle and was waiting for the captives outside. The wind ruffled the fur lining of his parka's hood as the Russian watched his Finnish comrades shove the prisoners across the lip of the tailgate.

The diplomat and his wife landed in snow two feet deep. They slipped and fell into the cold, wet carpet of dense snow. Hamilton raised his head and saw the blurred shapes of tree trunks through a veil of falling snowflakes. Everything else was white and barren.

"Nice quiet place, eh?" Kharkov's voice declared, the words barely intelligible above the howl of the north wind. "It is best to die in nice quiet place, don't you think?"

Hamilton glanced at the tops of Kharkov's boots, barely visible above the dense snow. He didn't look up at the KGB assassin, aware that Kharkov probably had a gun trained on them as they lay sprawled in the snow at his feet. Snow began to seep into Hamilton's clothing. Cold and clammy as death.

He wanted to tell Marsha he was sorry. He wished he could ask for her forgiveness and tell her one last time that he loved her. Hamilton turned to face her, more afraid of seeing hatred and betrayal in her expression than of the gun in Kharkov's fist.

Marsha's eyes met his gaze. She saw the pain in her husband's expression and understood the terrible emotions aroused by self-accusation and failure. But she felt only love and concern for Edward. She didn't blame him for what had happened or for not being able to protect them from their murderous abductors.

Edward Hamilton saw all that in his wife's eyes. He understood that she hadn't turned against him, despite what had occurred. They had devoted their lives to each other, and it seemed almost appropriate that they faced their final moments of life together.

Then Edward Hamilton felt a white-hot burst of pain at the base of his skull. The sensation ended a fraction of a second later, and Hamilton plunged into the mysterious oblivion of death. He was dead before he could hear the shot that killed him.

Marsha Hamilton died a moment later, when Kharkov pumped a second 9 mm bullet into the back of her skull. The Morkrie Dela assassin nodded with satisfaction and slid the pistol into a pocket of his parka. He turned to Olav and Larrs.

"You both did very well," Kharkov announced in Finnish. "Your contributions to the new order will not be forgotten."

"To kill Americans is enough reward," Olav replied with pride, his barrel chest swollen even larger as he stood stiffly at attention. "It is an honor to crush the enemies of the people's revolution."

"I know exactly how you feel," Kharkov assured him.

"I do not understand why we didn't simply kill them on the road along with the driver," Larrs admitted. "Why bring them all the way out here in the middle of a damn Lappi forest?"

"It is all part of a plan, young comrade," the Russian answered. "And you don't need to know any details about it at this time. Patience. I'll explain everything to you later."

"We trust you, Comrade Major," Olav declared firmly. "And we shall follow your orders without question."

"I'm so glad," Kharkov replied. "But right now we'd better get out of here before the snow gets too thick for the truck to get through. I wouldn't care to get stranded out here."

"We'd be lucky if we lived to see the next dawn," Larrs said grimly. "This is a very bad region. No one even skis in this area because there are no slopes and it is too far from civilization. Even the trees are dying out here."

"I know," Kharkov replied. "Olav chose an ideal site. We don't want the Americans to be found for a long time. As the mission progresses, I'll explain why. Now let's go, eh?"

The three men climbed into the truck, unaware that they were being observed by four wolves concealed by a snowdrift to the east. Incredibly keen ears and sensitive noses relayed more information to the animals than they acquired by sight, yet they waited until they could no longer see or hear the vehicle before they ventured from their observation point.

The truck rolled through the formidable snowdrifts and eventually vanished into the distance. The rumble of the engine faded, and only the scent of warm rubber, metal and exhaust fumes lingered in the air, along with the odor of the feared creatures that walked upright.

The wolves instinctively feared humans. They didn't fully understand the fear, but they obeyed its warnings. The strangeness of the creatures contributed to their caution, but a collective memory that had been passed down by their ancestors centuries ago further convinced the wolves that humans presented a special type of danger.

But the wolves were starving. The reindeer in the region were virtually extinct, and other natural prey were very scarce that year. The wolves had been lucky to find a vole or a mouse in the winter snow. None of them had been lucky for several days.

Now the warm, salty scent of fresh blood wafted from the site of the humans' visit to the forest. Fresh meat waited for the wolves. Although the smell of man still frightened the beasts, they approached slowly to investigate the two motionless figures sprawled in the snow.

They drew closer, and the smell of blood and fresh meat overcame their fear. The wolves soon discovered that the bodies in the snow offered no threat at all. They descended upon the meal with eager jaws.

**2**

The five men of Phoenix Force sat at the conference table in the War Room at Stony Man headquarters. Their attention was centered on the wide-screen television set at the end of the table. The scene was all too familiar to the five commandos. It was a sight that had become a hallmark of the dark side of the twentieth century.

The screen showed a public building that had been wrecked by an explosion. The windows were shattered; the doors torn from their hinges. The walls were cracked and crumbling. Flames danced inside the building, as if mocking the suffering of the human survivors being helped from the burning ruins. Bloodied and burned victims of the explosion were hauled from the wreckage by firemen, police officers and civilian volunteers. Men, women and children had been victims of the blast. Several bodies with blankets drawn over them were carried out on stretchers.

The clothing, the architecture and the cobblestone streets implied the incident had occurred somewhere in Western Europe, but such scenes had been documented everywhere in the world. Terrorism and senseless violence by fanatics and criminals had become an international plague. The barbarians didn't strike at soldiers on battlefields or even direct their attacks at politicians with whom they had some quarrel. They generally victimized innocent civilians simply to create an atmosphere of terror.

Phoenix Force specialized in dealing with such fanatics and butchers. They handled each situation as circumstances dictated. More often than not, that meant Phoenix Force had to respond to ruthless violence with deadly force that equaled or exceeded that of their opponents.

But Phoenix Force wasn't a "hit team." They weren't five killers working as the enforcement arm of Stony Man operations. They were a special commando team organized to deal with the most deadly adversaries of freedom, human rights and civilization itself. If they could take out opponents without resorting to deadly force, they did so, but wouldn't hesitate to kill if the situation demanded it.

They were professionals, the best antiterrorist assault team ever assembled, chosen from the cream of the crop in the field. The five best-trained and most experienced special operations experts in the free world comprised the unique and incredibly efficient unit known as Phoenix Force.

Hal Brognola switched off the television and VCR. Brognola was chief of operations for Stony Man. He took his orders directly from the President of the United States and determined assignments accordingly. Stony Man was super top secret, but unlike the CIA, NSA, FBI and other spook outfits, Stony Man didn't specialize in gathering and evaluating intelligence. They acquired such information from other sources and concentrated on taking direct action.

Brognola was the Atlas upon whose shoulders rested the entire burden of Stony Man. The top federal agent in the country had shouldered that Herculean task willingly from the beginning, and he intended to remain in charge until the end. Since the forces of extremist evil never rested, Brognola figured the end wouldn't come until long after he was dead and buried.

"What you've just witnessed happened a little more than six hours ago," Brognola announced as he stuck a cigar in his mouth. "The building housed a restaurant—hard to recognize what it was before the bomb tore it to pieces. It is located in the heart of Helsinki—the capital of Finland, in case your geography is a little rusty. Early reports state nine people were killed, five adults and four kids. About twice that number were injured by the explosion. Several of those are on the critical list with less than a fifty-fifty chance of surviving. A waiter got his arm torn off at the shoulder, a ten-year-old boy will have to have both legs amputated, and a woman passing by the place got a shower of broken glass in her face. She'll be blind for the rest of her life."

He slapped the file on the table with more force than he'd intended. Brognola nearly bit through the butt of his cigar. The fed had seen that sort of thing a thousand times, but it still filled him with anger and sorrow. The guy was the head of Stony Man because he cared, and that made the job even tougher.

"No point in going on with this," Brognola declared, looking at the five-man army gathered around the table. "You guys know more about the scum that do this than anyone does. And you know what happens to the victims."

"All too well," Yakov Katzenelenbogen replied with a nod.

Katzenelenbogen spoke from vast personal experience. The middle-aged Israeli didn't fit the Hollywood image of a commando warrior or a master spy, yet he was both. A cultured and well-educated man, Katz spoke quietly and thoughtfully. He was polite and often displayed a kindly smile.

There was nothing formidable about Katz's appearance. His iron-gray hair was clipped close to his skull. Katz stood less than six feet tall, was rather heavyset and a bit paunchy around the waist. The only unusual feature about Katz appeared to be his right arm. It had been amputated at the elbow, and a prosthesis was attached to the stump.

However, Yakov Katzenelenbogen was one of the most accomplished operatives in the history of espionage. His career had started when he was a teenager in Europe. The Nazis had rounded up most of the Katzenelenbogen family, but they failed to capture young Yakov.

His father had been a noted translator and linguist, and Yakov had been raised speaking four languages: German, French, English and Russian. As courageous as he was intelligent, Katz soon became a valuable addition to the French Resistance.

The American OSS later recruited Yakov for special missions behind enemy lines, and by the end of World War II, Yakov Katzenelenbogen was a seasoned veteran.

Katz then moved to Palestine and joined the battle for the independence of the state of Israel. He participated in many bloody campaigns in the Middle East, including the Six Day War. During that conflict, Katz lost his right arm due to an explosion that also claimed the life of his only son.

Yakov's skills became a valuable asset to Mossad, Israel's primary intelligence network. Mossad "loaned" Katz to other free-world intel organizations in return for favors from other spy networks. Katz had worked with the American CIA, the British SIS, the French Sûreté and the West German BND during his extraordinary career.

Promoted to colonel in 1973, Katz was placed in charge of Mossad antiterrorist activities in Western Europe. He was very successful in that role and might well have been promoted to head of Mossad, but Katz didn't wish to be a deskbound commander.

When he was asked to join Phoenix Force, the Israeli saw an opportunity to participate in the most unique elite fighting unit ever assembled. He realized he would never have another opportunity like that. Not at his age. Katz eagerly accepted the offer.

Stony Man couldn't have chosen a better unit commander for Phoenix Force. Yakov Katzenelenbogen was perfectly suited to the task, and the success of Phoenix Force proved it.

"I don't wish to sound callous about this, Hal," Katz began, taking a pack of Camels from the breast pocket of his tweed suit jacket, "but innocent people are killed and injured by lunatics like this every day. Sad fact, but true. We can't hunt every gang of fanatics in the world."

"Bloody well worth a try," David McCarter said as he rose from the table and started to pace. The tall, fox-faced Briton could never stay still for long, especially when something was bothering him. The video of the murdered and maimed civilians in Finland bothered McCarter a lot.

McCarter had been born and raised in the rough-and-tumble East End of London. Smart and tough, young David had always yearned for adventure. He joined the British army in search of that goal. McCarter found plenty of action with the Special Air Service. That suited McCarter just fine.

He served with the SAS in special operations in Northern Ireland, hunting down the most aggressive and ruthless terrorists among the IRA. His skill led to a tour of duty in Vietnam as a "special observer." He was actually attached to the Special Observation Group, which was a CIA front for clandestine operations behind enemy lines.

The SAS gave Sergeant McCarter plenty of new experiences. Some of these were on the familiar battlefields in the streets of Belfast. Others were in the hills and mountains of Oman during the 1970s. McCarter also participated in the famous and spectacular 1980 SAS raid on the Iranian embassy in London.

McCarter's hunger for action and his uncanny devotion to perfecting his combat skills made him an ideal candidate for Phoenix Force. An ace pilot, a champion pistol marksman, a superb survivalist and an expert in virtually every form of warfare, he had truly extraordinary talents.

The Briton had a short temper and a sharp tongue, and these sometimes got the better of him, yet he was otherwise a perfect fighting machine. His principles and patriotism balanced a personality that might otherwise have been antisocial and amoral. His intelligence and devotion to duty kept his thirst for action in check and prevented him from being a reckless daredevil.

"We'd all like to stomp out terrorism everywhere it exists," Katz assured McCarter, firing up his battered old Ronson to light a cigarette. "But that's hardly possible."

"I can dream, can't I?" the Briton replied with a shrug. "At least I can take some comfort in the fact that Hal wouldn't have shown us this little video unless it concerned our next mission."

"You got that right," Brognola confirmed, then paused to chew thoughtfully on his cigar. "The terrorist bombing at the restaurant in Helsinki today is the most recent of a series of events that has the President convinced it's time to send you guys to Finland."

"Would this have some sort of connection with that incident that occurred about a month ago?" Gary Manning inquired, gently rolling a mug of coffee between his palms. "I seem to recall reading in *Time* or *Newsweek* that an American diplomat vanished in Finland. Tiny little article, but I remember the guy's driver or bodyguard had been shot to death, and they figured the diplomat was kidnapped. His wife disappeared, too. Correct?"

"You've got a good memory, Gary," Brognola remarked, genuinely impressed. The fed opened the file folder. "The diplomat's name was Edward Hamilton, and his wife's name was Marsha."

*"Was?"* Manning raised his thick eyebrows. "Does that mean the Hamiltons are dead?"

"CIA, NSA and the State Department don't have much hope that they'll ever be found alive," Brognola replied. "No bodies have been found, but there were no ransom demands or efforts to negotiate a trade for the Hamiltons to get the release of terrorists or enemy agents from prison. Odds are they're already dead."

"Sure doesn't sound very promising," Manning agreed, sipping his coffee.

A ruggedly good-looking man in his mid-thirties, Manning was as muscular as a lumberjack from his native land of Canada. He was a quiet man and seldom spoke unless he felt there was a good reason to talk. Manning had always favored action over words.

Unlike McCarter, Gary Manning wasn't addicted to excitement. He was a perfectionist and possessed enormous resources of mental and physical stamina. Manning had always driven himself harder than most men. He put in more effort and he got more results.

Manning was never one to turn away from a challenge, which was probably the reason he developed the unique talents that had made him a candidate for Phoenix Force. While still a teenager, Manning had been intrigued by his uncle's demolition company. Explosives fascinated him, and he learned to handle everything from plastic explosives to improvised fertilizer bombs.

A hunter since childhood, Manning had perfected his skill with a rifle to become a top-notch marksman. He attended a military academy in Ontario, where his unusual abilities didn't go unnoticed. Lieutenant Gary Manning was a superb young officer in peak physical condition with a very high IQ and an uncanny expertise with both a rifle and explosives—the sort of young man who would be worth his weight in gold in a combat zone.

The only war available at the time was in Vietnam. The Canadian armed forces were not directly involved in the conflict, but the army sent him to Southeast Asia as a ''special observer.'' Manning was attached to the American Fifth Special Forces. He soon became a skilled sniper, an expert jungle fighter and a master of survival.

When Manning returned from Vietnam, he was contacted by the Royal Canadian Mounted Police. The escalation of international terrorism throughout the world had caused the Canadian government to consider the need for a special antiterrorist commando unit. The RCMP recruited Manning for this special team and sent him to West Germany to get on-the-job training with the GSG-9.

The West German antiterrorist unit was one of the best-trained professional teams of its kind in the world. Manning received his first taste of combat against urban terrorism in Germany. He worked with the GSG-9 for two years and returned to Canada to discover that the RCMP was no longer in the cloak-and-dagger business. Accusations of abuse of power had convinced the government to restrict RCMP activities and create the Canadian Security Intelligence Service to deal with covert matters.

The CSIS offered Manning a desk job, but the veteran warrior turned it down. He decided that if he had to be chained to a desk he might as well make a profit in the process. Manning became an executive for a major import-export corporation. He was rapidly promoted, thanks to his dedication and his determination to be the best at everything he did.

Manning probably would have remained with the firm to eventually become president of the corporation if he hadn't been recruited to serve in Phoenix Force. Manning believed that fighting terrorism and the international threats of organized crime and enemy sabotage was the most important work he could do. The Canadian was a workaholic and very good at his job.

"Does the President think there's a connection between the disappearance of the Hamiltons and the bombing of this restaurant?" Katz inquired, blowing cigarette smoke through his nostrils.

"He thinks it's possible," Brognola answered, checking the files again. "Both incidents are extremely unusual for Finland. It's a pretty stable country. Kidnapping foreign diplomats and terrorist attacks on public restaurants is a whole new phenomenon for Finland. Seems likely there's a connection."

"Crazy world," Rafael Encizo commented as he glanced at the circular scar in the center of his right palm. "And it's getting crazier all the time. There's no such thing as a safe place anymore. Maybe there never was."

Encizo had certainly never known a place of safety. A handsome, athletic man, Encizo appeared to be at least ten years younger than his forty-five years. He had experienced a lot of pain and hardship during his life, and he didn't believe the world was going to be any easier in the future.

Rafael Encizo had learned about the harshness of life at an early age in his native country of Cuba. Castro's forces had successfully seized power and established a new Communist state. The Encizo family had never been involved in politics, yet Castro's troops rounded them up.

Young Rafael joined a group of freedom fighters that vainly tried to launch a guerrilla war against the Communists, similar to Castro's own campaign against Batista. Unfortunately, the young and inexperienced counterrevolutionaries were no match for seasoned soldiers. Most of Encizo's band of rebels died in the hills in combat with Castro's troops. Survivors, including Rafael Encizo, fled to the United States.

On April 17, 1961, thousands of Cuban refugees returned in an abortive effort to regain control of their country. The Bay of Pigs invasion was a monstrous failure. Hundreds of counterrevolutionaries were killed by Castro's troops, and more than twelve hundred were taken prisoner. Rafael Encizo was among the captives.

Encizo was taken to the infamous El Principe, Castro's political prison. He was starved, beaten and tortured in an effort to "reeducate" him, but the jailers couldn't break him. However, Encizo eventually pretended to surrender to their wishes. The guards grew careless with their prisoner, and one of them paid for his mistake with his life. Encizo snapped the man's neck and escaped.

He returned to the United States and became a naturalized citizen. Encizo worked in various unusual occupations and developed equally unique skills. He

had been a scuba instructor and a professional bodyguard. He had dived for sunken treasure in the Carib-
bean and assisted federal agents in missions against
drug smugglers. Employed as an insurance investiga-
tor specializing in maritime claims when called to a
meeting at Stony Man headquarters and asked ᴛo join
Phoenix Force, Encizo hadn't had to think twice
about his answer.

"Today's terrorist bombing is proof that things are
going from bad to disastrous in Finland," Brognola
explained, leafing through the file folder. "Mr. Hamilton, along with his wife, isn't the only diplomat to
vanish in Finland recently. The West German ambassador disappeared two weeks ago. A visiting member
of the British parliament vanished during a tour just
five days ago. The most recent disappearance appears
to have occurred two days ago. A Swiss buyer was in
Helsinki to arrange a major purchase of paper products. He just vanished. The authorities aren't sure he
was kidnapped, but they figure there's a pretty good
chance that's what happened."

"Sounds like a Bermuda Triangle for foreign visitors from Western democracies," Calvin James
mused. "All these missing persons are from the U.S.
and countries of our allies, right?"

"Bingo," Brognola confirmed.

"That's not much, but it's something," James remarked, tapping the tips of his long ebony fingers together thoughtfully. "Maybe I'm still inclined to think
like a cop, but I like patterns and whoever the bad guys
are, they seem to have an MO in progress."

Calvin James was the only member of Phoenix
Force who hadn't been selected by Mack Bolan when

the unit was first created. James had been drafted by Phoenix Force to assist in a mission against the Black Alchemist terrorist outfit. The original fifth member of the team, Keio Ohara, had been killed during the assignment, and James had remained with the unit ever since.

A tall, slender black man who received his first lessons in survival on the South Side of Chicago, James had been born and raised in a tough environment. At seventeen, he enlisted in the United States Navy and became a hospital corpsman with a SEAL team. His Sea, Air and Land unit saw plenty of action in Vietnam, and Calvin James was right in the middle of it.

He left the service with a number of decorations for valor and an opportunity to continue studying medicine and chemistry under the GI Bill. He had planned a medical career until his mother and kid sister became victims of the growing crime rate. That event steered James toward law enforcement.

James joined the San Francisco Police Department and eventually became a member of the Special Weapons And Tactics squad. James was in the process of carrying out a SWAT operation when Phoenix Force contacted him and enlisted him for the Black Alchemist affair. Calvin James had found an outfit he felt he really belonged with, and there was no place he would rather be.

"The trouble with the pattern is that the bombing of the restaurant doesn't seem to fit," Brognola told James. "A bunch of Americans and West Europeans vanished. No ransom demands. Nobody taking credit for the kidnappings. But somebody *is* taking credit for the restaurant bombing."

"That's interesting," Manning remarked. "Who?"

"Somebody claiming to be the Democratic Liberation League for the Republic of Finland, DLLRF," Brognola answered, checking his notes to be certain of the title. "Newspapers, television and radio stations all received phone calls from a person taking credit for the bombing and claiming this league was responsible. The Finnish parliament and several embassies all got phone calls with the same story."

"Did the bastards say why they did it?" McCarter inquired, still pacing the floor like a nervous lion in a circus cage.

"The caller claims the league blew up the restaurant to get the attention of the Finnish government," Brognola explained. "They claim they want Finland to sever all trade and diplomatic relations with the Soviet Union. They want the Finnish Communist Party to be outlawed, and they want an end to what they describe as 'Finland's gradual decline into Marxist socialism.' Last, but not least, they also demand stronger ties with the United States and the democracies of Western Europe and Japan. And they want NATO missile sites established to protect Finland from the Soviet Union."

"Great," James muttered. "Just what America needs. Terrorist groupies for a cheering section in Finland."

"I don't see how this is connected with the kidnappings," Encizo began. "The abductions appear to be of people the terrorists claim to support."

"Unless," Katz said thoughtfully, "the bombers aren't supporters of pro-Western democracies. The incident at the restaurant isn't going to make anyone

very sympathetic toward the demands of the so-called
'Liberation League.' Could be someone has decided to
try some reverse psychology in Finland.''

"You might be right, Yakov," Brognola agreed.
''Uncle Sam and Finland aren't getting along too well
since Hamilton and his wife vanished. State Department has been bitching at the Finnish government to
find the couple. The ambassador has been giving them
more flak. The governments of Great Britain and West
Germany have been on Finland's back, too. The Swiss
will probably be on their case next. Of course, they
haven't found any bodies yet, and there isn't any proof
of foul play except for the murdered embassy driver.
Frankly, that isn't going to get one-tenth the amount
of attention that this restaurant bombing will get.''

"Sure isn't going to improve America's image
abroad," Manning commented. "Sounds like foreign
relations are already going to hell in a hand basket.''

"You got it," Brognola confirmed. "Between nag-
ging the Finnish parliament about missing persons and
this terrorist incident by supposedly pro-West zealots, the United States and our allies are gonna be
about as popular as a turd in a punch bowl. The
President's administration isn't winning any popular-
ity contests with the American public right now,
either.''

"The administration screwed up," James said
sourly.

"Don't they all?" the fed replied with a shrug. "The
fact is, this isn't a good time for the President to get
involved in a series of denials and groping explana-
tions concerning radical activity in Finland. You know
how politicians are. They worry more about their

public image than anything else. All the rest can go on the back burner for a while until they can clean the egg off their faces. There may not be that much time left to stop the situation in Finland from boiling over. If that happens, it sure isn't gonna help this side of the Iron Curtain."

"So when do we leave?" McCarter asked eagerly.

"Can you be ready to go in two hours?" Brognola asked.

"We can be ready in one," Katz assured him.

**3**

"Mission accomplished, Comrade Colonel," Major Anatoliy Mikhailovich Kharkov announced, a wide grin plastered across his face. "Two more imperialists from the West have disappeared. Helsinki may soon be known as the Scandinavian Beirut, eh?"

"I do not find that amusing, Comrade," Lieutenant Colonel Sergei Georgeovich Bajanov replied as he sat at a small desk in the office of a warehouse in Kotka. "You find too much pleasure in the taking of human life."

"I simply follow orders," Kharkov replied with a shrug. "Orders that you give me, Comrade. You are actually criticizing me for doing what you instructed me to do. Is this logical?"

"Your attitude disturbs me," Bajanov told him. "This assignment is a delicate operation, although it requires ruthless tactics. Lives must be taken, but this must be done with surgical care to maintain the balance of action and counteraction."

"I feel no regrets about killing enemies of my country," Kharkov replied with a sigh as he took out his cigarettes and stuck one in his mouth. "We have a kind of war in progress with the Americans and their capitalist allies. People get killed in wars. I am simply a soldier who kills on covert battlefields, eh?''

"You're a killer without a conscience," Bajanov said in disgust. "Unfortunately, there is a use for creatures such as yourself in the KGB. A limited use."

"Not so limited for this mission," Kharkov replied smugly, sitting in a chair facing Bajanov. "You are Department Eleven, Comrade Colonel. So you are in charge, but we both know this is basically a Morkrie Dela operation. Without me, nothing would have been accomplished."

"Your services are surely appreciated by Moscow," Bajanov said, unable to keep the contempt from his voice.

Bajanov realized it was unwise to make an enemy of Kharkov—or whatever the KGB's killer's real name was. The Morkrie Dela division lied about everything, including the names of its personnel. The assassination section of the KGB was a very shadowy and secretive outfit, feared even by the other members of the Komitet Gosudarstvennoi Bezopasnosti, the Committee for State Security. Murder came easily to men like Anatoliy Kharkov. The assassin could decide to kill Bajanov if the colonel pushed him too far.

Of course, that was highly unlikely. Whatever else Kharkov might be, he was a field-grade officer in the KGB and a professional espionage agent. Kharkov was not stupid, and he wouldn't act harshly if doing so would endanger his own status within the Soviet spy network.

Bajanov also realized Kharkov was little more than a tool for the interests of the KGB. In fact, that description suited Bajanov, as well. He hadn't requested his present assignment in Finland, and he didn't care much for the mission or the individuals he was forced to work with.

Sergei Bajanov had been recruited by the KGB upon graduation from a military academy near Leningrad in 1958. He had followed orders with loyalty and skill. Although Bajanov had risen within the ranks of the KGB, his youthful idealism had vanished with the passing of time and the experiences of life. He realized that the sword-and-shield emblem of the KGB was less than accurate. As often as not, the KGB was the aggressor and not merely the protector of the Soviet people.

Still, Bajanov didn't intend to defy the Kremlin. The only principles he believed in were those of personal professionalism and the survival and comfort of himself and his family. Bajanov had a wife and three children in Leningrad. They enjoyed a much higher standard of living than most Soviet citizens. Bajanov wasn't about to jeopardize their safety or their position among the favored few of the USSR by incurring the wrath of Moscow.

"Why do you seem displeased, Comrade Colonel?" Kharkov inquired, blowing a ring of gray smoke at the ceiling. "Our mission has been a total success thus far. Every phase has been carried out without flaw, and the stupid Finns have responded exactly as we'd desired."

"I'm concerned that we might be overconfident," Bajanov answered, waving the smoke away from his face. He had quit smoking five years previously and hated the smell of cigarettes. "How did you dispose of the bodies?"

"The two we disposed of today?" Kharkov replied. "We handled them the same as the others. Took them up to Lapland and killed them in the forest. Left the bodies in the snow for the wolves to have for dinner."

"Wolves?" Bajanov frowned.

*"Da,"* Kharkov laughed. "Olav and Larrs noticed wolf tracks in the snow. They used to be poachers, so they're familiar with the footprints of the beasts in that region. The wolves don't have much prey in that area, so the bodies of our dead enemies are no doubt a welcome addition to their diet."

"I don't want you and those two Finnish apes to kill any more foreign diplomats," Bajanov declared. "There have been enough disappearances to upset the United States and the other democracies involved. We need to concentrate on the next phase of the mission."

"Terrorist sabotage," Kharkov said, a trace of distaste in his tone. "I don't like dealing with fanatics. They're unstable and unreliable."

"We can agree on that, Comrade," Bajanov said with a nod. "But using the local extremists reduces the danger that the Soviet Union will be directly linked with the recent unpleasant events taking place in Finland."

"I realize that," Kharkov assured him. "I also realize many of those right-wing zealots would turn on *us* if they knew we were manipulating them. Remarkable how easy it has been to convince these dolts to play right into our hands."

"If you want a terrorist, you find a fanatic," Bajanov stated. "The sort of fanatic who only believes

in violence and destruction as a means of creating social change. Such individuals are eager to accept any
reason to destroy and kill. Give them a cause and a
target, and they'll do the rest with little coaxing.
Frankly, it makes little difference whether they choose
to call themselves left-wing or right-wing. They're all
irrational, so they don't need rational reasons for their
actions."

"Amazing," Kharkov remarked with a sly smile.
"We're turning potential enemies into allies for the
world revolution of international communism. This
country has long been a thorn in the side of the Soviet
Union, but soon it will be a new ally."

"The plan could go wrong if we're careless," Bajanov warned. "Afghanistan was supposed to be an
easy victory. Too much happened too soon, and all of
it was directly linked with the Soviet Union. I don't
need to remind you that things have not gone so
smoothly for us in Afghanistan. Moscow most certainly does not want another situation like that to deal
with."

"This time will be different," Kharkov stated.
"And you and I will be rewarded for our glorious ac-
complishments during this mission, eh?"

"I just want to do the job and go home," Bajanov
told him as he turned to stare out the window.

He had a telescope mounted by the window. The
view overlooked a harbor, and the Gulf of Finland
extended beyond the piers and fishing vessels. With
the help of the telescope, Bajanov could sometimes
locate Gogland Island or even Moshchnyy Island.

These islands were Soviet properties. Bajanov wondered if he could paddle a rowboat across the gulf to
one of the islands. Home was so close, yet—until the
mission was over—so very far away.

"We'll be going home soon," Kharkov assured him
as he rose from his chair and moved to a file cabinet
across the room. He reached for a bottle and glasses
set on the top of the cabinet. "Let's drink to our success, Comrade Colonel."

Kharkov noticed that the liquid in the bottle was as
clear as water. The label was written in Finnish and
bore a familiar emblem of two reindeer, horns locked
in combat. Kharkov smiled.

"At least these Finns have good vodka," Kharkov
declared as he opened the bottle. "Almost as good as
Russian vodka, eh? Last year I was stationed in the
People's Democratic Republic of Yemen as an ad-
viser. Training terrorists how to kill. It is a terrible
country—even if it is a Marxist state. Islamic country, you understand? The Koran forbids Muslims from
drinking alcohol, so you can't get any good vodka
there. Finland is a much better place to be stationed."

"Finland won't be a very pleasant country much
longer," Bajanov said grimly. "We are planting the
seeds of chaos. The Finns will find a harvest of terror
and destruction before the present government falls."

"To be replaced by a new government more agree-
able to our leaders in Moscow," Kharkov said cheerfully, pouring vodka into two glasses. He handed one
to Bajanov. "Then Finland will finally join the en-
lightened nations liberated by the Soviet Union."

"I doubt that the Finns would appreciate how lucky they will be," Bajanov remarked as he took a deep drink of vodka. The colonel had been unable to keep a trace of sarcasm from his voice.

## 4

Even Phoenix Force occasionally encountered problems with transportation. Hal Brognola tried to pull enough strings to arrange a direct flight from the U.S. to Finland, but the only available plane was a Finnair flight from Seattle, and Brognola couldn't manage to get clearance to transport special weapons and equipment on the plane—not without compromising the security of the mission.

Rather than waste time wheeling and dealing for the next Finnair flight, Brognola arranged a military transport to Frankfurt, West Germany, for Phoenix Force. Thanks to contacts in U.S. Army Intelligence, Brognola set up a covert plane trip for the five elite commandos and their gear. Phoenix Force had friends within the BND, the West German equivalent of the CIA, who helped them get a secure Lufthansa flight to Helsinki, Finland.

When they arrived at the airport, the five warriors were glad they hadn't taken a direct flight from the United States. Groups of demonstrators were scattered throughout the terminal, and larger crowds had gathered around the entrance of the airport. They carried signs written in Finnish, Swedish and English bearing slogans such as Go Home Americans and Stop American Imperialism.

Uniformed police and airport security officers had their hands full keeping the crowd at bay. The policemen held back several demonstrators within the terminal as the members of Phoenix Force passed through the halls toward the baggage claim section. Three protesters broke through the police barricade to rush toward the five men. They probably suspected Calvin James and Rafael Encizo weren't German nationals.

"Damn America!" a long-haired youth snarled in thickly accented English. "No want you come in Finland!"

*"Je ne comprends pas,"* James replied with a distressed expression. *"Parlez-vous français?"*

*"Nej,"* the young man replied, obviously embarrassed, then proceeded with what James took to be an apology or explanation.

The three protesters backed away to be grabbed by some policemen who shoved them into the crowd. Phoenix Force continued to walk to the baggage claim area. Tourists were busy trying to locate their belongings along the conveyor belts that deposited suitcases and trunks from the baggage collectors outside. People muttered in half a dozen languages, complaining about missing luggage and discussing the hostility displayed toward Americans.

Phoenix Force headed for a door labeled Airport Security in six languages. A tall man with wavy silver hair and a heavy lantern jaw greeted them at the door.

"Good afternoon. Are you the gentlemen from Canada?"

"We sent some special tools and equipment from Frankfurt," Katz replied. "Do you know where they might be?"

"Let us discuss it, gentlemen," the man invited. "Please come in and make yourselves comfortable."

Phoenix Force entered the small office, which was furnished with a metal desk and three chairs. A small computer terminal sat on a table.

The man with the silver hair closed the door and locked it. He smiled at the five visitors. "I always feel silly using these passwords they come up with," he declared. "I am Orm Karista of the Security Intelligence Agency of the Republic of Finland."

"We're the five businessmen from Canada," Katz told him, offering his left hand.

"A pleasure to meet you," Karista stated, shaking Katz's hand. He glanced at the Israeli's right hand and wondered if it was a prosthesis. Katz wore a five-fingered device that was covered by a glove and appeared quite lifelike. "I assume you noticed the demonstrators."

"Yeah," Encizo remarked. "Sort of an 'unwelcome wagon' for visiting Americans."

"I"m sorry to say you'll see a great deal of that attitude in Finland right now," Karista said with a sigh. "The so-called Democratic Liberation League has taken credit for another act of terrorism. It happened less than six hours ago. A bomb exploded in a school. Nine children injured. Three children and a teacher were killed."

"Jesus," Gary Manning said, shaking his head.

"What reason did they give for this bombing?" Katz inquired, taking a pack of Camels from a jacket pocket.

"The terrorists claim it was a bloody protest against teaching Swedish and Russian in our schools," the Finnish intel agent explained. "Swedish is the second official language here in Finland, spoken by about seven percent of the population. The DLLRF claims Swedish causes a 'cultural division' and 'linguistic confusion' within Finland."

"Some demonstrators approached us in the terminal," Katz remarked. "One of them said some anti-American rubbish in broken English."

"I replied in French, and that convinced them to back off," Calvin James added.

"The young man made an apology," Katz continued. "Now, I know only a smattering of Swedish and even less Finnish, but I believe the youth spoke Swedish."

"The Swedish-speaking minority are among the most outraged by these terrorist actions," Karista explained. "The restaurant that was bombed earlier served Swedish dishes, and most of the patrons were Swedish Finns. Not surprisingly, the Swedes feel they're targets of these DLLRF terrorists."

"Rather looks like they're right," David McCarter commented. The British ace felt awkward and half-naked because he wasn't armed. "Has our crate been brought in yet?"

"It's behind the desk," Karista replied. "You'll find a crowbar back there, too."

"Thanks, mate," McCarter said as he headed for the crate.

"I'm curious about what you fellows have in there," the Finn admitted. "It's not full of weapons, is it?"

"I sure hope so," Encizo remarked as he joined McCarter in prying open the crate.

"I don't understand," Karista began. "The SIA has already arranged special firearms permits, and we could supply you with anything you need."

"Whenever possible, we like to use our own weapons," Katz explained, "weapons we're familiar with. Guns we've fired on a target range, if not in actual combat. We know what to expect from these weapons, and they feel more natural in our hands. Knowing your weapon makes a big difference in combat."

"You gentlemen talk as if you expect to have shoot-outs with the terrorists," Karista said with a frown. "This is Helsinki, not Chicago in the Roaring Twenties. Blazing gunfights aren't done here."

"How about bomb attacks that murder women and children?" Calvin James asked dryly. "That's been goin' on, hasn't it? I'd say a nice honest gun battle with the terrorists would be a great improvement."

"That's difficult to argue with," the Finn admitted. "But you must understand my concern for the safety of civilians and the security of my organization. The SIA has agreed to cooperate with your group because the President of the United States personally requested this. Finland wishes to cooperate with the United States of America. We are allies."

"We appreciate your situation," Katz told him. "I assure you that we share your concerns, Mr. Karista."

"Don't forget, the reputation of the United States and her allies is on the line, as well," Gary Manning added. "To be honest, we're here because American interests are involved. Finland is located along the Soviet border. That makes this country's future very important to us."

"American interests aren't too popular right now," Karista replied. "I'm glad you have Canadian passports. That may make matters considerably easier for you. Since the terrorists claim they want NATO missiles in Finland, I don't suggest you make any statements supporting the North Atlantic Treaty Organization in casual conversation."

"Don't worry," Katz replied. "Finland has to remain officially neutral toward both the U.S. and the Soviet Union. Its very survival depends on that. Putting missile sites here could cause more trouble than it would be worth. The Soviets would certainly respond by escalating their own missiles along the border, and they'd probably increase activity in Cuba and Central America to set up new missile bases there."

"Yeah," James commented. "The arms race is already a nightmare waiting to come true. No sense in making it any worse."

"No one will argue with that," Karista said with a nod. He noticed McCarter and Encizo removing two submachine guns from the crate and placing the weapons on the desk. Both men were busy checking pistols, working the slides, inspecting the barrels and trigger mechanisms before inserting magazines.

"They get a little eager at times," Katz commented, barely glancing at the pair. "Is there any new information about the diplomats who have vanished recently?"

"Yes," the Finn answered. "We think we know where the bodies have—"

The bellowing roar of an explosion outside the office interrupted Karista. Phoenix Force reacted to the noise instantly. Manning and James moved to the door. The Canadian carefully turned the knob and opened the door a mere crack while James flattened his back against the wall, and gestured at McCarter and Encizo to toss him a weapon.

The Briton had already thrust a Browning Hi-Power autoloader into his belt and grabbed an Ingram M-10 machine pistol from the desk. McCarter headed for the door while Encizo gathered up a Beretta Model 92SB and shoved in a magazine before tossing the pistol to Calvin James. The black warrior caught the Beretta and quickly worked the slide to chamber the first round. Katz had stepped to the desk and took a SIG-Sauer P-226 pistol from the crate. Encizo slid a Heckler & Koch P-9 autoloader into his belt and slipped his arm through the shoulder strap of an H&K MP-5 machine pistol.

Orm Karista was stunned by how quickly and smoothly the mysterious team of strangers responded to the sound of danger outside the office. Each man seemed to know exactly what to do and what his teammates would do. No one got in the way of anyone else as they quickly prepared for trouble. Whoever these men were, Karista realized, they functioned like a well-oiled machine. They had obviously worked together many times in the past and were accustomed to stressful and dangerous situations.

"Got a bunch of alarmed tourists," Gary Manning reported as he peered out the door at the people clustered around the baggage claim area. ''None of the people I can see appear to be hurt, but they're all looking down the hall and upward. Explosion must have happened on the floor above us.''

''What's on the next floor?'' Katz inquired as he braced the SIG-Sauer in the gloved prosthesis and worked the slide with his left hand.

''Airport shops,'' Karista answered, drawing a Lahti Model 35 pistol from shoulder leather. The Finnish autoloader resembled a Luger P.08, but the Lahti was a better combat weapon than the better-known German pistol, which is more prone to jam in an emergency. ''Newspaper stand, gift shops, a coffee shop, barber shop.''

''Why would the terrorists set off a bomb here?'' James wondered aloud as he thrust the Beretta into his belt.

''There are a lot of anti-American demonstrators at the airport,'' Gary Manning remarked as Encizo tossed him a Walther P-5 autoloader. ''Maybe they're the terrorists' target.''

''Press is probably going to give this a lot of coverage,'' Katz added. ''No doubt television cameras from several countries were shooting footage of the demonstration. Terrorists like television coverage when it suits their purposes.''

The rattling of automatic weapons echoed from the halls of the terminal. Karista cursed under his breath and chambered a round to his Lahti. Encizo and McCarter reluctantly replaced their subguns on the desk.

''What are you doing?'' the Finn demanded. ''Those scum are shooting up there!''

"Terrorists don't care if they shoot innocent by-standers," Encizo explained. "We do."

"We can't use automatic weapons in a crowded public place," McCarter said, continuing the explanation. "That M-10 of mine is too damn indiscriminate about what it shoots. We'll have to rely on pistols."

"Masters, Sanchez and Johnson," Katz began, addressing McCarter, Encizo and James by their current cover names. "Go for the stairs at the top of the hall. The rest of us will find another way up there. Any ideas, Karista?"

"Yes," the Finn intel agent replied with a nod. "Follow me. I'll get you there."

THE BOMB HAD EXPLODED in the coffee shop. A harmless-looking package wrapped in brown paper had been left under a table by a polite young man dressed in a long overcoat. The man paid his bill, thanked the lady behind the counter and wished her a nice day before departing. Two minutes later, the package exploded.

The blast had virtually destroyed the coffee shop. Tables and chairs had been reduced to charred rubble. The bloodied bodies of customers were sprawled across the floor, and the lady at the counter lay dead with chunks of pastry scattered around her lifeless form. Windows had shattered and exploded outward, and three passersby screamed as shards of glass tore into their flesh. Others bolted with cries of terror from the carnage. An elderly woman was bowled over and trampled by the panic-stricken crowd.

The young man who had left the bomb in the coffee shop smiled as he watched the human stampede from the safety of the barber shop. He turned to two other young men who were seated in the shop leafing through magazines. The barber had been clipping the hair of a French tourist when the explosion occurred. He had been alarmed by the blast, but suddenly discovered even more cause for concern.

The three young men suddenly produced weapons from their winter coats. Two of the men brandished Danish-made Madsen Model 1950 submachine guns with folding metal stocks, while the third aimed a French MAB autoloading pistol at the barber and his customer.

*"Merde!"* the Frenchman exclaimed.

The pistol that had been made in his homeland snarled, and a 9 mm parabellum slug punched into his chest and drilled a lethal cavern through the heart. A scarlet stain appeared on the white sheet across the Frenchman's chest. The cloth became an impromptu shroud as the customer slumped dead in the chair.

The barber raised his hands in surrender as the gunman stepped closer. A cruel smile slithered across the assassin's smooth young face as he raised the MAB and shot the barber point-blank in the face.

Two airport security officers and three police officers detailed for crowd control rushed into the hallway to investigate the explosion. The two gunmen with Madsen choppers covered their faces with black ski masks and charged from the barber shop, immediately opening fire.

The law enforcement officers didn't have a prayer. Twin streams of full-auto 9 mm rounds slashed into uniformed torsos without mercy. Only one police officer managed to draw his pistol before a trio of bullets smashed into his chest. The five officers collapsed in a twitching heap, and the gunmen fired another volley of Madsen slugs into the dying men.

Three more terrorists appeared at the east end of the hallway. The panicked crowds had been spurred to greater haste by the thundering chatter of the submachine guns. They were even more upset and frightened when the second trio of masked terrorists appeared: two men and a woman, although the female's bulky coat and baggy trousers served to conceal her gender somewhat. All three were armed with Madsen subguns.

The female terrorist and one of her male companions opened fire on the fleeing crowd. It was cold-blooded murder. Icy cold. Parabellums tore into backbones and ruptured hearts and lungs. Unarmed civilians dropped like tenpins as blood streamed across the smooth floor in slick red puddles under the feet of the terrified survivors.

*"Ruma sika!"* the murderous bitch spat as she hosed the helpless victims with 9 mm slugs.

*"Poliisi!"* several voices cried desperately.

Two policemen responded to the plea, but their path was blocked by the crowd stampeding blindly through the halls, too terrified to realize the cops were trying to penetrate the human tide to offer rescue. The officers held their Lahti pistols high, muzzles pointed at the ceiling, to avoid threatening the bystanders. They struggled against the violent flow of the crowd, reluctant to shoot until certain of a target.

The terrorists observed no such restrictions and opened fire. The Madsen subguns blasted lethal messengers into the two policemen and three unfortunate civilians. Blood spewed from a dozen terrible wounds. The victims slumped to the floor, their lives flowing from them while others screamed in helpless terror.

McCarter, James and Encizo reached the head of the stairs to the floor where the terrorist slaughter was in progress. They saw the bombed remnants of the coffee shop and the bullet-riddled corpses of the five uniformed officers.

By then the crowd had been driven from that portion of the hallway, making the work of the three Phoenix Force commandos less complicated. Although there were no innocent bystanders to worry about, the trio still faced the problem of dealing with the terrorists who remained in the hall. Two of them had just reloaded their Danish chatter guns. A third still lurked in the barber shop, out of sight from the stairwell.

"I hate pitting pistols against submachine guns," Encizo commented in a philosophical whisper as he crouched behind a pillar at the head of the stairs. "Especially when the other side has the submachine guns."

"We could run down and get ours, too," McCarter said with a shrug, covering the Browning in his belt with his jacket. "Of course, that would give these bastards enough time to kill a dozen more people. I'll get their attention."

"There's not much cover out there," Calvin James noted, surveying the area with a frown.

"Well, that works both ways," McCarter replied, displaying his faith in the SAS motto: He Who Dares Wins. "Those blokes won't have much cover, either."

"So far they haven't needed it," Encizo muttered as he gripped his H&K P-9 autoloader.

The Cuban had never used that particular pistol in an actual firefight before. He had formerly carried a Walther PPK or a Smith & Wesson Model 59 as personal side arms in combat. Encizo trusted weapons made by Heckler & Koch and had long favored the MP-5 and other full-auto firearms, so it evolved naturally that he would eventually carry a pistol of the same manufacturer. He had done well with the P-9 autoloader on the firing range, but right then he wished he had a gun more familiar to his grasp in actual battle conditions.

Calvin James shared the Cuban's apprehension. He had formerly carried a .45 caliber Colt Commander, but the men of Phoenix Force had recently decided that all their primary weapons ought to be chambered for 9 mm parabellum. The logic of that was difficult to argue with, because the 9 mm cartridge is available virtually anywhere in the world and is used by the military and police of most nations outside the United States.

It also made sense that all the side arms and subguns used by Phoenix Force be chambered for the same caliber. Thus they would be able to exchange ammunition in an emergency. James had reluctantly left his trusted Colt on the shelf and tried several 9 mm pistols before choosing the Beretta 92SB as his new side arm. But the pistol was untried by James in fiery combat.

James and Encizo felt a twinge of envy for Mc-
Carter, who carried the same model Browning 9 mm
pistol that he had favored for years. They stopped en-
vying the Briton as he stepped into the hall with his
hands raised and empty.

"Hey, you blokes!" McCarter shouted at the two
startled terrorists. "Where the hell is the loo around
here?"

The enemy gunmen were amateurs, and they hesitated for a moment due to surprise rather than reluc-
tance to kill an unarmed man. McCarter took
advantage of that split second and dived to the floor
in a rapid shoulder roll. His body tumbled twice and
landed behind the shallow cover of the corpses of the
slain policemen.

The terrorists triggered their Madsen subguns. A
sheet of 9 mm slugs slashed through the corridor.
Most of the bullets burned air above McCarter's prone
form. A few smacked into the lifeless flesh of the dead
cops, but none found the Briton.

Encizo and James quickly aimed their pistols while
the terrorists concentrated on McCarter's position.
The Cuban commando squeezed the trigger of his
H&K P-9 and fired two rounds into the upper torso of
the closest opponent. The terrorist's body buckled
from the impact of the high-velocity projectiles.

The wounded terrorist tried to turn his Madsen
subgun toward Encizo's position. The Cuban shot him
again, pumping a third round into the gunman's
throat. The bullet severed the spinal cord and burst
vertebrae before tearing an exit wound at the back of
the man's neck. He collapsed, dead before he hit the
floor.

Calvin James fired his Beretta a split second later. His target was about two yards farther than Encizo's target. The terrorist had also started to move and re-direct his Madsen to point it at Encizo's position. James's shot missed the center of the man's chest, the parabellum tearing tissue in the terrorist's left biceps.

The gunman howled and triggered his weapon, his body convulsing from the pain. The Madsen rose with the recoil, as the terrorist was unable to control the subgun he held in one hand. A burst of 9 mm rounds raked the ceiling. Fluorescent tubes shattered as bullets popped out the ceiling lights overhead.

"Die, bastard," James rasped as he rapidly fired two more rounds.

The bullets hit the gunman in the chest, left of center. Crimson holes appeared in the terrorist's shirt-front as the man's coat flapped open. James had placed the two slugs close together, and both bullets had torn into the enemy triggerman's heart. His life pump totally shattered, the man dropped to the floor, too dead to even manage a death twitch.

The surviving terrorist in the barber shop had seen his comrades fall, and held his fire. After all, his partners had been armed with submachine guns and now lay dead. He was armed only with a MAB semi-auto pistol and obviously had less of a chance.

James and Encizo stepped over the top of the stairs, pistols held ready. They looked around with quick, darting glances, wary of unseen opponents who might be lurking nearby. In fact, they heard the chatter of automatic weapons farther down the hallway. That meant there were more terrorists involved in the assault. McCarter remained behind the shelter of the slain policemen, using the corpses as improvised sandbags. The Briton had drawn his Browning Hi-Power and held the pistol in a two-hand Weaver's grip.

Suddenly the female terrorist appeared at the end of the hallway, her Madsen submachine gun pointed at Encizo and James. Encizo was still close to the stairs and quickly ducked behind the archway at the mouth of the well. James had advanced a few yards by the time the gun-packing woman appeared. He jumped through the open door of a gift shop an instant before she opened fire.

Bullets whined against the floor and sparked on the concrete edge of the archway to the stairs. Stray rounds smashed a window pane of the gift shop. James ducked low as shards of glass spewed overhead. A woman screamed inside the store. A sales-clerk was crouched down behind a counter along with two customers. They had chosen to stay under cover after the bomb exploded instead of trying to flee with the others. With the firefight in progress, they were no doubt questioning the wisdom of their decision. All three were women. Only one screamed, and the others muffled her cries, fearful the gunmen might hear her.

"It's okay," James called to the hidden civilians. He hoped one or more of them understood English or at least that the tone of his voice offered some reassurance. "I'm not gonna hurt you. I'm here to help."

The female terrorist shrieked with anger because she had failed to shoot either Encizo or James. She fired another volley at the stairwell. The triggerwoman hadn't noticed David McCarter stationed behind the pile of corpses in the hall.

The Briton aimed carefully and squeezed off two shots. The killer female stood almost fifty feet from McCarter's position, a fair distance for an accurate shot with a handgun under a high-stress situation. However, McCarter thrived on excitement and functioned best under pressure. The Briton was also a superb marksman with a pistol.

McCarter's first bullet drilled into the woman's chest. Her torso rocked from the impact, and the second 9 mm round tore into her solar plexus and burrowed upward to rip into her heart. She fell, her Danish subgun falling from her twitching fingers and skidding across the floor.

The pistol-packed terrorist in the barber shop fired his MAB autoloader at McCarter's position. Fortunately for the Phoenix warrior, the enemy gunman didn't possess the Briton's skill. The MAB bullets fell short of the intended target. Two slugs ricocheted off the floor. A third struck the lifeless flesh of a corpse near McCarter's position, and the body jerked from the impact.

McCarter swore as he rolled away from the corpse.

While the gunman was concentrating his efforts on trying to take out McCarter, Calvin James ventured out from the gift shop. He remained close to the columns of the storefronts and surreptitiously crept toward the barber shop. He saw the barrel of the terrorist's MAB pistol extend from the mouth of the shop. It was still pointed at McCarter's position, as if the gunman had completely forgotten James and Encizo.

Bastard probably had, James figured. He had noticed in past encounters with terrorists that a common character trait among them seemed to be dogmatic single-mindedness. They tended to set their sights on one goal, one target, and ignore the rest of the world.

The gunman hadn't noticed James's stealthy approach. The black warrior considered his options. If possible, he wanted to take the guy alive for interrogation, but couldn't afford to risk his own life or the lives of his partners.

The terrorist triggered two more shots at McCarter's position, blasting hot lead into the uncaring flesh of another dead policeman. James saw the slide of the enemy's MAB pistol lock back in place to reveal the empty chamber. The man had burned up all his ammo.

Fate appeared to provide James with the opportunity to seize a prisoner. He rushed to the barber shop before the terrorist could eject the spent magazine and reload the MAB handgun. James bolted across the threshold and deftly chopped the butt of his Beretta across his opponent's wrist to strike the French pistol from his hand.

The MAB fell to the floor as the terrorist, more surprised than hurt, uttered a startled yelp. The hard-ass from Chicago then swung the barrel of his Beretta at the masked face.

The terrorist dodged the attack, and the steel frame of the pistol whistled harmlessly past the gunman's right ear. The Phoenix pro realized his error and mentally cursed himself. He had violated one of the primary rules of combat survival. He had underestimated his opponent.

The terrorist seized James's arm and twisted his wrist as if wringing out a wet towel. The Beretta autoloader dropped from James's open fingers. Calvin James had been disarmed, but he was far from helpless. A second *dan* belt in tae kwon do, he still had his body for a weapon.

He thrust a back kick into his opponent's belly. His boot heel caught the man hard between the navel and gonads. The terrorist gasped in choking agony and doubled up from the blow. James easily broke free of the man's weakened grip and promptly pumped an elbow stroke to his opponent's jaw.

James followed with a cross-body karate chop aimed at the side neck, intending to render the man unconscious with a blow to the nerve center at the neck muscle, but fate had another surprise for the commando. The terrorist's head had snapped backward from the impact of the elbow smash, and the side of James's hand struck the man across the neck and crushed the thyroid cartilage.

The gunman stumbled backward, both hands clutching his wrecked throat. The eyes bulged and seemed to poke from the holes in the ski mask. A dark stain appeared on the black cloth at the portion covering the man's mouth. The terrorist wilted to the floor, trembled slightly and lay still in the absolute calm of death.

"Hell," James said with a sigh. "Well, I tried to take him alive. Guess you can't expect all your plans to work out all the time."

ORM KARISTA HAD LED Yakov Katzenelenbogen and Gary Manning to an exit. They stepped outside to be whipped by a strong, chilly wind laced with thousands of snowflakes. Alarmed crowds had gathered outside, and the police were busy trying to keep the curious away and escort to safety the people who were pouring through the exits in panicked streams. The police realized they had to get the bulk of the civilians out of the building before they could launch an organized assault on the enemy gunmen inside. The shoving and grasping of terrified people hastily trying to flee the terminal made the task all the more difficult.

Karista located the police captain in charge and showed him SIA credentials. Katz and Manning couldn't hear Karista converse with the captain because of the screaming masses of fear-filled humanity, but they wouldn't have understood more than a handful of words, anyway.

Karista turned to the Phoenix pair.

"He's agreed to let us enter the building," the intel agent explained. "And he'll order his men to keep out and allow us to handle the situation as we see fit. Actually, I think he's relieved that someone else has volunteered to take care of this task. After all, the poor fellow had no idea something like this might happen. He and his men were prepared for some overzealous demonstrators, not terrorists armed with automatic weapons."

"We hadn't expected to encounter anything like this so soon, either," Manning assured him, removing a thick silver fountain pen from his coat pocket as he spoke. "We're not really prepared for this sort of thing, either, but we've had lots of experience at improvising in the field."

"Looks like they've gotten most of the civilians out of the section we're concerned with," Katz observed as he watched two policemen hustle a small group of tourists through a door. "Let's go teach the terrorists some manners."

"I hope you know what you're doing," Karista commented, reaching inside his coat for his Lahti pistol.

"Don't pull that thing out of leather until we get inside," Katz instructed. "Flashing guns about out here will only serve to alarm the onlookers worse than they already are. Don't forget, three of our friends are in there. Be certain of your target before you open fire."

"I'm not an amateur," Karista replied, clearly offended.

"Have you ever been in a gun battle before?" Katz inquired, well aware that most intelligence operatives have very little experience with violence.

Karista frowned and didn't answer Katz's question, but his failure to reply was itself an answer. In fiction, secret agents might squeeze a lot of cold triggers and warm thighs, but in reality an intelligence officer is more apt to be evaluating information from wiretaps or spying on suspects with infrared telescopes while squatting on a rooftop or crammed in the back of a surveillance vehicle. Karista had never fired his weapon except at paper targets at SIA pistol ranges.

"You stay behind us and back us up," Manning told Karista as he pulled at both ends of the fountain pen to reveal a narrow red ring at the center. "Do what we tell you, and don't try any heroics. You might get somebody else killed, as well as yourself. And if you see me throw this pen, cover your eyes.''

"What is it?" the Finn asked, staring at the fountain pen.

"Variation of a magnesium flare," the Canadian explosives expert explained. "It'll burst into a brilliant white light when detonated. Bright enough to temporarily blind anyone who looks directly at the glare."

"Let's go before the terrorists have time to move to the opposite side of the airport," Katz declared as he headed for the entrance.

Manning and Karista followed. The doors led directly to the hall where the terrorists had struck. The chatter of automatic weapons, mixed with the *bang-crack* of 9 mm pistols, revealed that the other three members of Phoenix Force were already engaged in battle with the enemy.

Few civilians remained in the corridor. Three were elderly individuals who had been knocked down and trampled by the panic-stricken mobs in their desperate charge for the exit. Two other civilians had been wounded by terrorist bullets but still struggled to reach safety. The others who remained were dead.

Katz and Manning unsheathed their pistols as they ventured into the hallway. Karista followed their example and drew his Lahti autoloader. They advanced slowly, moving close to the walls for cover.

The trio approached the shops and discovered five civilians pursued by a masked figure armed with a Madsen submachine gun. The triggerman was about to fire when he spotted Katz, Manning and Karista.

He started to turn his weapon toward the Phoenix pair and their Finnish ally.

Katz and Manning held their fire. Too many civilians were in the killground, too many innocent bodies that might fall victim to stray bullets. Manning hurled the pen down and turned his head to avoid looking directly at the painful nova of white light exploding from the floor. Katz and Karista shielded their eyes as well.

The gunman and two civilians screamed as the magnesium flare erupted. The flash lasted less than a second, but the light was bright enough to fill their eyes with the painful glare. One of the tourists cried out that he was blind. He was right, but the effects of the flare would last only a minute or two. The glare wasn't powerful enough to cause lasting damage to human retinas.

The terrorist didn't understand what had happened. He covered his eyes with one gloved hand and held the Madsen subgun in the other. If he had dropped the gun, he would have been taken prisoner. Since the man still presented an immediate threat, Gary Manning aimed his Walther P-5 and opened fire on the blinded opponent. The Canadian triggered the double-action autoloader twice and blasted two 9 mm rounds through the side of the terrorist's head. The man's skull burst open and smeared blood and brains across the glass pane of a shop window.

The gunman's body collapsed to the floor, his Danish subgun clattering on the hard surface. The civilians screamed and threw themselves to the floor, fearful that more bullets would be sizzling through the tension-filled air. The two blinded bystanders stumbled about helplessly.

"Karista!" Katz shouted as he advanced. "Stay here and protect these people!"

"Right," the Finn replied with a nod, finding the hunt for the remaining terrorists more nerve-racking than he had imagined.

The two Phoenix warriors continued to move through the hall and gradually approached the center of the mall area, where James, McCarter and Encizo had clashed with the enemy. The air smelled of burnt gunpowder and fresh blood. The corpses of more civilians and uniformed police and security guards littered the corridor.

*"Seis!"* a voice hissed from the archway of a rest room.

Katz and Manning turned toward the sound and discovered a masked figure in the archway. The terrorist held a woman close to his chest, his arm locked around her neck and the muzzle of a compact pistol pressed against the side of her head. The woman was shaking, and her eyes opened wide as she stared at the two commandos. Her lips trembled in mute pleas for rescue.

"Easy," Katz said, lowering the SIG-Sauer in his left hand. "The bastard has a hostage."

"Could take him out with a head shot," Manning whispered, the Walther still ready in his fist.

"He might still shoot the hostage," Katz muttered. "Leave him to me. You check the rest of the corridor and see if our friends are okay. I'll take care of this clod."

"Yakov..." Manning began, reluctant to leave his partner.

Katz ignored him and stepped toward the terrorist and the female hostage. The man snarled something in Finnish. Katz wasn't sure what had been said, but assumed he was being warned not to come any closer. The Israeli stopped, bent his knees and lowered the SIG-Sauer to the floor.

"There," Katz began, straightening his legs and raising both hands to shoulder level. "Is that better?"

The man still held his pistol threateningly against the woman's skull. He glanced at Manning, expecting the Canadian to attempt an attack while Katz distracted him. Manning was tempted to do exactly that, but he suspected Katz had a plan, and he had learned considerable respect for the Israeli's opinions. The Canadian reluctantly moved down the hallway and disappeared around a corner.

"Does that make you happy, you stupid little savage?" Katz inquired as he stepped closer.

*"Seis!"* the terrorist repeated, shifting the gun away from the woman's head and in Katz's direction.

Katz's right hand jutted forward, and he pointed the gloved "fingers" of the prosthesis at his opponent's face. The cloth at the end of his index finger burst apart. A .22 Magnum hollowpoint slug with a mercury core crashed into the terrorist's forehead, exploding on impact with bone. Metal and bone shards tore into the man's brain. He was dead before he could hear the crack of the high-velocity bullet breaking the sound barrier.

The slain terrorist slumped to the floor, pulling the woman down with him. She screamed hysterically, shocked by the events and the blood staining her face and clothing. Katz pried the dead man's arm from her neck and helped the woman to her feet. She struggled blindly, but the Israeli embraced her to hold her firmly yet gently.

"It's over," he whispered kindly, unsure if she understood his words but hoping that the tone of his voice would reassure her that she was no longer in danger. "It's all over now."

The woman stopped struggling and began to weep. Katz held her and let her cry into his shoulder until she had exhausted the tears caused by the tumbling emotions of fear, repulsion and relief. The other four members of Phoenix Force arrived as Katz gently released the woman. She wiped at her tears and looked up at Katz, saying something to him with a shaken voice.

He smiled and nodded in reply. The woman headed for the entrance to the hall while Katz turned to his companions. He pulled the glove off his right "hand." The fingers of the prosthesis were made of steel, and the index finger was actually the barrel of the single-shot .22 Magnum pistol built into the device. A wisp of smoke rose from the black muzzle at the end of the digit.

"I see you handled the situation okay without us," Manning declared, thrusting his Walther P-5 into his belt.

"I ruined another pair of gloves," Katz said with a shrug. "Ought to start buying these things by the gross. Any terrorists left?"

"Pretty sure we got 'em all, unless some noncombatants managed to slip away," McCarter replied. "Didn't manage to take any prisoners."

"Not surprised," Katz remarked. "These clowns were definitely graduates of the mad-dog school of terrorism, but I doubt that they could have told us much."

"Would be nice if we knew where to start looking for the enemy," Encizo commented with a sigh of regret.

"Maybe Karista can help us with that," Katz replied. "I sure hope so, anyway. If this sort of terrorism continues much longer, Finland will be in utter chaos and the United States is going to be very unpopular in this part of the world."

**5**

The Finnish Security Intelligence Agency satisfied the police that the terrorists had been taken care of by personnel from their organization and that the local authorities would be given necessary details when such information was no longer a threat to national security. The police weren't terribly happy with the state of affairs because they realized they would probably never get the truth about what happened at the airport. However, they were relieved that the slaughter had been stopped and not too upset about the fact that none of the gun-wielding fanatics had survived. Six policemen, three airport security officers and more than a dozen civilians had been murdered, which didn't leave much sympathy for the terrorists.

Orm Karista and the men of Phoenix Force gathered together in Karista's office, located on the tenth floor of a modern building. The building housed several law firms and insurance agencies. The SIA had set up a front for internal operations by masquerading as an insurance corporation with a very exclusive clientele. The headquarters of the Finnish intel agency was little more than a figurehead because it was far too easy for the KGB to gain information from the SIA head office. Most of the important covert matters were handled by safehouse operations like the one headed by Karista.

Yakov Katzenelenbogen peered out a window. The office had a nice view of the National Opera Theater. Katz enjoyed the opera, although he seldom had time to attend. He doubted that he would get an opportunity to see a performance while he was in Helsinki. Pity, he thought as he closed the curtains.

"Now," he began as he turned to face Karista, "you were about to tell us about the missing diplomats before we were interrupted by the terrorists back at the airport."

"Yes," Karista said with a nod, moving to a file cabinet next to an IBM computer. "The remains of two bodies were found in a remote forest region in Lappi, the largest province of Finland and the most northern. I have the details on file here."

"Have the bodies been identified?" Gary Manning inquired, helping himself to a cup of freshly brewed coffee. It was very thick and very strong, just the way Manning liked it.

"Yes," Karista answered, taking a diskette from the files. He fed it into the computer as he spoke. "The bodies belonged to Roger Tillman, a minor official in the American diplomatic corps with the United States embassy, and the other is believed to be his brother, Robert Tillman, who disappeared at the same time."

"Was Robert also with the diplomatic corps?" Rafael Encizo asked as he watched Karista call up a file and check the information that appeared on the screen.

"No," the Finnish intel agent replied. "Robert Tillman was just a tourist. Apparently he was here to visit with his brother. We believe whoever abducted him mistakenly believed both men were with the American embassy.''

"How were they killed?" Calvin James asked.

Karista consulted the screen. "Both victims had been shot in the back of the skull by a 7.65 mm pistol. Very exact bullet placement through the fourth ventricle and into the medulla oblongata. Each shot severed the spinal cord and destroyed the midbrain simultaneously.''

"Professional," Katz commented thoughtfully. "The killer is probably an experienced executioner.''

"Why is the SIA certain of the identity of Roger Tillman, but they haven't been able to identify the brother positively?" Encizo inquired.

"Because Roger was identified by his dental records," Karista explained. "Robert's dental records aren't on file at the American embassy. We've contacted the American branch of Interpol at the Justice Department in Washington, D.C., and requested copies of Robert Tillman's dental records.''

McCarter frowned, then asked, "Were the bodies mutilated?''

"Very badly," Karista confirmed. "The medical examiner isn't certain, but he suspects the Tillman brothers had been partially eaten by either wild dogs or a pack of hungry wolves.''

"Wolves?" Manning said with surprise.

"Oh, yes," Karista said with a nod. "There are a few packs of wolves left in Lappi. Nobody is quite sure how many. Any wolves in that area would be pretty hungry. This has been a hard winter, and it is particularly bad up in the Lappi province.''

"Is it possible there are more bodies up there?" James inquired.

"The Tillman brothers are the most recent kidnapping victims, and their corpses were discovered by accident," Karista answered. "A couple of trappers stumbled across the bodies and reported the discovery just this morning. It's quite possible there are more bodies up there. It is a very remote area. No reason for anyone to go there."

"Unless one wants to get rid of some bodies and needs a place where they won't be discovered for a while," Katz commented as he tapped his prosthetic steel "fingers" against his left palm. "No one has taken credit for any of these abductions, correct?"

"That's right," the Finn confirmed. "We're getting a lot of heat from the governments of the United States, England, West Germany and Switzerland because these individuals vanished, but no terrorist outfit or organization of any sort has taken credit for these kidnappings. In fact, a common rumor suggests none of these abductions were real. This popular notion suspects that the American CIA and the British secret service faked the abductions."

"Bloody hell," McCarter snorted, jamming a Player's cigarette in his mouth. "Where did they get a silly idea like that?"

"Because a lot of people suspect the CIA or some similar organization of the Western nations trained the terrorists who have been blowing up public establishments here in Helsinki," Karista explained. "This idea is especially popular among the Swedish communities, since Swedish Finns have been the most plentiful of the victims."

"That's crazy," James muttered, shaking his head in dismay. "It doesn't make any sense."

Katz lit up a Camel. "This whole business is beginning to make sense," he corrected. "The masterminds behind both the abductions and the terrorism know exactly what they're doing. They kidnap American, British and West European diplomats in order to get those governments irritated with Finland. Then they send out terrorists who appear to be pro-American and pro-NATO to carry out attacks on civilians. They favor the Swedish minority because most minority groups tend to feel they're picked on by the majority—whether that's strictly true or not. Put it all together, it's a very clever plan."

"And it sure sounds like the sort of thing favored by a certain Soviet outfit we've crossed swords with several times in the past," Encizo commented with a nod.

"KGB," Manning said grimly.

"That's whom we suspect, too," Karista told them. "Trouble is, we don't have any proof. All the evidence points in exactly the opposite direction—toward the United States and her allies."

"It would be pretty foolish for the Soviets to point the finger at themselves," Katz stated. "With these tactics, the KGB is making the Western nations more hostile toward Finland and the Finnish people more hostile toward the United States and other NATO countries. The natural evolution of this will be a tendency to be more willing to deal with the Soviets and— I'm sure the KGB is hoping for this—more sympathy toward the Communist Party here in Finland."

"Well, we Finns don't care much for communism," Karista said, somewhat defensively. "Stalin's armies tried to invade Finland in 1939 until 1944. The Soviets failed to take our country. Stalin claimed control of several other nations, but he couldn't take Finland. We're very proud of that part of our history, and we're not apt to surrender our democracy to the Communists."

"But there is a Finnish Communist Party?" Manning asked.

"There is also an American Communist Party; a British Communist Party," Karista replied stiffly. "And the largest Communist Party in Western Europe is found in Italy...."

"You're quite right," Katz assured him. "We're not finding fault with your country, Mr. Karista, far from it. As a matter of fact, I'd be disappointed in Finland's concept of a free society if communism was outlawed here. Freedom of choice is what a multiparty system is all about. I don't object to a system that allows Communists to voice their opinion, but I strongly oppose a system that allows *only* the Communist point of view."

"Such as the Soviet Union," Manning added.

Karista smiled weakly. "I'm sorry if I overreacted. Of course, there is a Communist Party in Finland. Actually, the Party was illegal for more than ten years. Finland suffered from Communist terrorism as early as 1918, when terrorists murdered and plundered civilians for almost a year before being defeated. Communism was outlawed sometime in the 1930s and wasn't legalized until 1947. That was an agreement Finland made with the Russians after the armistice at the end of the so-called Russo-Finnish War."

"Bloody history lessons," McCarter muttered sourly.

"Let the man explain this as he sees fit." The Phoenix Force leader cast a hard glance at the Briton. One of these days, Katz thought, we have to get McCarter fitted for a muzzle.

"Communists have actually held a few minor positions in some government coalitions," Karista continued. "But communism is not popular in Finland, and party membership has never been very large, and it's actually been decreasing since 1979. Oh, the Soviets have tried to influence our people in the past to try to get us to adopt communism, but it has usually backfired and made us all the stronger opposed to that system."

"That explains why the KGB has decided to try a different and more radical tactic this time," Manning commented. "Reverse psychology. They make the U.S. and the Western NATO nations appear to be the villains and thus make themselves appear to be the good guys."

"Might work, too," James added. "Even if it doesn't, a lot of innocent people could get killed before it's over."

"A lot of innocent people *have* been killed," Karista reminded him.

"This is just the beginning," Encizo warned. "Things will get a lot worse if we don't stop these sons of bitches. But where do we start?"

"The terrorism has occurred here in Helsinki," Katz replied. "We start here."

"There might be some vital evidence in that forest region in Lappi," Manning declared. "If we can find more bodies, we might also find some clues about who is responsible."

"The weather is a bit nasty this year," Karista warned. "The temperature has been averaging about minus ten degrees up north, and the snowfall has been very heavy."

"Minus ten isn't so bad." Manning shrugged. "I've been in colder weather than that while on hunting trips in Canada."

"All right," Katz agreed. "But make it a brief trip. I don't want our team strength diminished for more than twenty-four hours."

"If I don't find anything after searching for eight hours, it probably means I wouldn't find anything if I searched for a week," Manning said with a nod. "Get somebody to fly me up there. I'll look around for a few hours and come back whether I find anything or not."

"Somebody ought to go with you," Katz declared.

"Sounds like a waste to me," McCarter snorted.

"Don't look at me," James commented. "I had too many Chicago winters to volunteer to play Eskimo."

"I'll go," Encizo announced. "Sounds a bit like some salvage operations I've worked on before. Different setting, same basic principle."

"I'll arrange for a plane and pilot," Karista stated. "And I'll send an SIA agent with you, too. Someone who speaks the Lappi dialect as well as English. You might need him if you happen upon any witnesses in the region."

"Sounds good," Manning agreed. "What are you guys going to do while we're up north?"

"I think we'll look for some people to push," Katz replied with a thin smile. "And see who pushes back."

**6**

Gary Manning, Rafael Encizo and Rolf Lautanen arrived at the airstrip. It was located between Helsinki and Vantaa. Literally hundreds of small airfields scattered throughout Finland provide transportation within the country. Finland is roughly the size of the state of Montana, and most of its population of five million are located in the southern provinces. Travel to the uninhabited regions of the north is a bit more difficult.

Lautanen didn't resemble the popular stereotype of a Finlander. He stood less than five and a half feet tall and was slightly built with round shoulders and a narrow chest. His black hair and brown eyes were as dark as Encizo's, but his complexion was pale, as if he had spent most of his life indoors—which, in fact, he had.

"Are you gentlemen from the insurance firm in Helsinki?" a tall man with long blond hair and a tawny mustache inquired as he met the three visitors at the gate to the airfield.

"That's right," Lautanen replied, pushing the fur-lined parka hood back from his head. "You must be Sven Skraddare."

"I'm Sven," the blond confirmed, extending his hand. "Pleased to meet you. I understand you all speak English?"

"Sure makes things easier for us if we all speak the same language," Manning admitted, shaking Sven's hand. "Is the plane ready?"

"Yes," Sven assured him, flashing a set of even white teeth. "I've taken care of everything. Just climb aboard and load your belongings, and we'll be ready to go."

Karista had said that Sven Skraddare was efficient and reliable. The SIA employed him on a part-time basis when they needed a pilot for courier missions that required his skills. A twenty-seven-year-old Swedish Finn, Sven had worked for the SIA for five years and had proved his loyalty.

The snow continued to fall as they walked to a twin-engine Beech with amphibious landing gear. The Phoenix Force pair carried backpacks loaded with cameras, sample bags and a few meager supplies just in case the plane was delayed by the weather and they were forced to remain in Lappi longer than anticipated.

All four men were dressed for cold-weather conditions. Actually, the climate in Finland is generally milder than most would suspect of a country located so far north. However, this winter had been particularly cold, and the snowfall was greater than usual. Of course, the northern province of Lappi would be much colder than the southern areas, and the men had prepared accordingly.

Manning, Encizo and Lautanen settled into the rear of the plane with their gear while Sven started the engines. The Beech soon headed down the snow-laced runway. The amphibious gear handled the slippery surface with ease, and the plane rose smoothly into the twilight sky.

"I think we should have waited until morning," Encizo commented, checking the buckle to his seat belt. "We'll have a better chance of finding evidence when it's light."

"Morning won't help us," Lautanen explained. "Lappi is close to the arctic zone and experiences approximately two months of continuous night at this time of year. In the summer, between May and July, Lappi has continuous daylight. In the Soviet Union they refer to this as the white nights."

"In Alaska they call it the midnight sun," Manning remarked. "Too bad it isn't summer. Our job would be a lot easier if we didn't have to search the forest with flashlights."

"Don't expect it to be much of a forest," Lautanen warned, inserting a cigarette into his mouth. "The area is notoriously barren. Not quite tundra, but about as close to it as you'll ever wish to see."

"That doesn't sound terribly encouraging," Encizo said with a sigh.

"But it might not be so bad," Manning told him. "The lack of trees and bushes might mean fewer hiding places to check out. Maybe we'll find what we're looking for with greater ease due to the bleak nature of the terrain."

"We don't even know what we're looking for," Encizo muttered as he glanced out a window at the dim sky blurred by sheets of falling snow. "You really believe all that crap, or are you just trying to sound optimistic?''

"A little optimism couldn't hurt," the Canadian replied, although even he had doubts that it could help.

MAUNO TAIVAS WATCHED the plane disappear from the view of the window of a hangar. He smiled with satisfaction. He had overheard Sven's conversation with the three strangers. They had all spoken English. Damn CIA, Taivas thought with loathing. Just as he had suspected.

Taivas had been employed as a mechanic at the airfield for six months. He knew that Sven Skraddare was a part-time operative for the Finnish Security Intelligence Agency, but neither Sven nor the SIA suspected Taivas was a "cutout" agent working for the KGB. He was registered as a Social Democrat, but Taivas had secretly belonged to the Communist Party since he was a student in college.

Not that Taivas was openly involved in efforts to support the Communists in Finland or get any of the party candidates elected. He considered these efforts absurd. Taivas knew his countrymen were too prejudiced against communism to choose that system of government unless drastic actions were taken to encourage the change.

Taivas had been an ideal recruit for the KGB. A fanatic who mistook extremism for idealism, he believed the goals of his beloved cause justified any methods used to accomplish them. He was quite eager to assist KGB activities within Finland. Taivas regarded the Soviet Union as the great liberator, the righteous opponent of imperialist oppressors and defender of the people's revolution throughout the world.

He didn't think he was betraying his country by working for the KGB. Taivas considered himself a patriot fighting for a cause that he thought of as more important than the desires of his fellow Finns. More important than the life of any individual or the lives of innocent people. After all, his zealot's mind rationalized, millions would die in a full-scale nuclear war, and the only hope for world peace was international communism, with the USSR in charge of maintaining order. The Soviets certainly seemed to have a knack for that role.

Taivas had been ordered by the KGB to get a job at the airfield and spy on Sven. However, nothing had happened worth reporting until now. Taivas had installed an eavesdropping device in Sven's telephone, and he had monitored the pilot's calls for months before the call came from the "Helsinki insurance firm" asking Sven to prepare his plane for an emergency flight to Lappi.

The spy realized that the KGB was responsible for the disappearance of several diplomats from Western nations. Taivas also suspected the bodies had been disposed of in Lappi, because the KGB was particularly interested in anyone who wanted to arrange a sudden trip to the northern province.

Taivas had decided to strike a blow for the cause. He didn't want to simply spy on Sven. The pilot was just an unprincipled lackey, in Taivas's opinion. He wasn't really the enemy, but SIA agents and the CIA were another matter. Taivas figured the KGB would be delighted if he took out Sven and his capitalist masters.

So Taivas had planted a small explosive device in the engine of Sven's plane. It was a crude device. Taivas had never received formal training in espionage or sabotage, but he had learned how to construct a simple time bomb from a would-be anarchist he had known in his college days. Taivas smiled as he checked his wristwatch. The device was due to explode in twenty minutes, and the plane would crash somewhere in the Lappi region.

He could hardly wait to relay this information to his current KGB control officer. The Soviet agent would certainly be surprised by his resourcefulness, Taivas thought, and he would certainly be promoted to a more important position within the revolution.

THE BEECH CONTINUED TO FLY into the dark, snow-streaked sky. The farther north the plane traveled, the darker the sky appeared. Sven Skraddare calmly operated the controls as he gazed through the windshield at the flurry of white flakes. The pilot had flown in far worse conditions, and a little snow didn't worry him in the least.

"We'll be approaching your destination in a few minutes, gentlemen," Sven called out to his passengers. "I hope I can find a decent place to land. Is this an area with a lot of hills or trees?"

"Not according to the description," Rolf Lautanen answered. "The area is supposed to be fairly level from dense snowfall. Few trees or large rocks to present any problems in landing this amphibious plane."

"I'd feel more confident if you had actually seen this place and knew about it firsthand," Sven admitted. "Hey, dudes. What do ya think of my English?"

"Excellent," Manning replied. "In fact, I've noticed a lot of people in Finland speak superb English."

"Many Finns learn English in school," Sven explained. "It helps a lot with business if you speak at least three languages in Finland. Of course, Finnish and Swedish are the most important languages for dealing with our own people, but English is very useful when dealing with the nations of the West. Most European businessmen speak English—except the French, and Finland doesn't do much trade with France."

"We do more trade with the Soviets," Lautanen commented, his tone suggesting he was a bit embarrassed to admit that fact. "That's part of our efforts for neutrality. With the Russians at our border, it is advantageous for Finland to maintain good trade relations with the Soviets."

"Geography can present one with undesirable neighbors," Encizo remarked. "But it is still best to get along with your neighbors as much as possible."

"You understand our predicament," the SIA agent said with a nod of appreciation. "Finland is in an awkward position. We are determined to remain a free people with a democracy, but we have to remain on good—or at least nonhostile—terms with the Soviet Union. Our military is restricted to only just over 40,000 members, thanks to the Treaty of Paris, signed in 1947. Those restrictions don't apply to the Russians, of course. The USSR has the largest military force in the world, with close to four and a half million personnel.''

"I can see why Finland—'' Manning began, but his statement was interrupted by a loud bang vibrating against the metal framework of the plane.

The Beech suddenly swerved and shuddered from the impact of the explosion in the engine in the right wing. The bomb had been placed in the manifolding, and the blast effectively wrecked the stators and the engine fan, smashed the cooling system and burst the engine's protective cone. The remnants of the engine began to burn.

"*¡Cristo!*" Encizo rasped as he glanced out and saw the flames dance along the wing. "We're in deep trouble.''

"Sven!" Lautanen cried. "*Tuli!*''

"*Ja!*'' the pilot replied sharply. He switched to English. "I know there is a fire. Worse, we lost a wing engine, and one engine isn't going to keep us airborne. We're going down. Brace yourselves. We'll probably land hard.''

The Beech whirled and cut a crazy pattern in the air as it began to descend. The angry buzz-saw whine of the remaining engine screamed in their ears. Their stomachs twisted into knotted fists, and their hearts hammered as if a deranged drummer were attacking each man's chest from within. Their vision became a wild blur as the plane spun and tumbled while it plunged toward the white carpet below.

Sven struggled with the control levers and worked the rudders with his feet. Sweat flowed down the pilot's face as he tried to raise the nose before the plane crashed into the frozen ground.

He succeeded, but the Beech sailed toward a cluster of spruce trees. Sven tried to guide the plane past the abbreviated forest. The lack of the right engine reduced the plane's ability to maneuver. It refused to turn to the right while it hurtled forward. The left wing smashed into the trunk of a spruce tree. Metal groaned, and the mounting beam of the wing snapped. The root rib gave way, and the wing snapped from the carriage of the plane.

The amphibious landing gear touched the ground. It slid smoothly across the snow, but the crippled craft was totally out of control. Sven desperately held onto the levers, although he realized there was nothing he could do. The Beech slid across the white surface like a low-flying missile. The pilot couldn't alter its route or slow its fearsome momentum.

Sven prayed aloud, reverting to Swedish as terror robbed him of his other linguistic knowledge.

God didn't help him, unless one considered a large gray boulder a divine gift intended to halt the progress of the airplane. The nose of the Beech slammed into the rock barrier. The canopy collapsed, and the windshield shattered. Sven opened his mouth to scream, but the wreckage suddenly closed in on him like a great metal fist.

Encizo, Manning and Lautanen convulsed with the violent impact of the crash. Their heads and limbs bounced like those of a rag doll at the end of a string. Manning's safety belt burst open, and the Canadian was flung from his seat. He smashed into a cabin wall and slid senseless to the floor.

Enicizo heard Lautanen moan in agony, but couldn't see what had happened to the SIA agent. The Cuban's head had recoiled violently, and his entire body trembled from the aftermath of the collision. Black mists drifted across his consciousness. Encizo was vaguely aware of the smell of something burning, but he was too groggy to appreciate the importance of the situation.

The right wing continued to burn, and the fire began to spread to the carriage of the crippled plane as the fuel tanks leaked a steady stream of gasoline onto the ground.

## 7

Helsinki might be the city that the designers of Washington, D.C., had dreamed of building. The wide streets are surrounded by hundreds of parks and gardens. The architecture has an open and spacious feeling, which is reinforced by use of the local light-colored granite. The city has a long and remarkable history. Helsinki was founded in 1550 by Gustav I Vasa, king of Sweden when Finland was a duchy under Swedish rule. The city has witnessed many historical events and experienced frequent hardships.

Largely destroyed by retreating Swedish forces in 1713 during the Northern War between Sweden and the Russian Empire, Helsinki was rebuilt by 1809 during the rule of Czar Alexander I. When Finland gained independence in 1917, Helsinki was made the capital. In 1952 Helsinki was the site of the Olympic Games and the signing of the historic Helsinki Accords of 1975, which was the conclusion of the Conference on Security and Cooperation in Europe, formed to promote economic stability, peace and human rights. Thirty-two European nations, the United States, Canada and the Soviet Union are members of the CSCE.

Yakov Katzenelenbogen considered these facts as he sat in the back seat of a black sedan driven by a Finnish intelligence agent named Kalevi. The Phoenix Force commander wondered what the world would be like if nations signed formal agreements and actually lived up to the terms of these deals. Treaties and pacts seemed to be nothing but worthless paper that never prevented wars or hostile invasions. They certainly did little to stop terrorism.

Of course, that was the reason Phoenix Force had been created. Governments, conventional law enforcement and military organizations were unable to deal with certain kinds of problems. As long as the modern Vandals threatened the safety of civilization and the survival of freedom, Phoenix Force would remain in business.

"We're close to the very heart of Helsinki," Kalevi announced, steering the sedan around a minibus that had stopped in the middle of the street. Kalevi clucked his tongue in disgust as he passed the other vehicle.

"Tourists," the SIA agent muttered, shaking his head and glancing at the occupants of the minibus. The driver and passengers appeared to have stopped their vehicle to argue about a street map spread across the dashboard. "Where do people learn to drive like this?"

"Ever been to Boston?" Calvin James inquired. Twilight had fallen, but he still noticed a magnificent building in the distance. "That's really somethin'. What is it?"

The structure was indeed impressive. A long set of marble stairs extended from the column of Doric pillars in front of the building. Three domed roofs stood atop separate towers, the largest and tallest in the center. Ornate spires were mounted at the peak of each cupola.

"Yes, it is something," Kalevi agreed. "That's the Suurkirkko, the Great Church. Lutheran church, of course. Most Finns are Lutherans. If you get a chance, you ought to visit the Senate Square. The State Council Building is located there, as well as the Suurkirkko and the University Library, designed by Karl Ludwig Engel, the most breathtaking work of that world-renowned architect."

"I've heard that the Senate Square is the most beautiful city square in the world," Katz commented, but he didn't crane his neck to get a better look at the Great Church. Phoenix Force wouldn't have any time to indulge in sightseeing while they were in Helsinki. There was no point in getting his hopes up that he would get to see the square under better conditions.

"That's very true," Kalevi confirmed with obvious pride. "The Town Hall at Kungsholmen in Sweden, the Stroget in Copenhagen, Red Square in Moscow—all are ugly and drab compared to our Senate Square."

"Wonderful," David McCarter muttered without enthusiasm. The Briton didn't want to hear about the architecture of Helsinki. He was eager to get back into action again. "Is it much farther?"

"We're almost there," the SIA agent assured his passengers, steering onto Pohjoisesplanadi. "See that building that resembles a post office? That's the tourist information center. That means we're very close."

"Has Sanders—the NSA man—someone in the tourist center?" Katz asked.

"Of course," Kalevi said with a grin. "The National Security Agency likes the spot, and so do we. So does the KGB, I suspect. We all have interest in who plans to visit Finland. Surprising how much intelligence can be acquired by such methods. I've done work like that in the past. Terribly boring, but a lot of intelligence operations are boring. I suppose you fellows know about that."

"We're lucky," James replied. "We don't get any jobs that are dull."

The sedan pulled into the underground parking lot of a small motel located two blocks from the tourist information center. They emerged from the sedan and mounted three flights of stairs. On the second floor, Kalevi led them to a door marked with the numeral 22. He knocked twice, and a voice from inside the room told him to enter.

Kalevi turned the knob and pushed the door open, revealing a heavyset middle-aged man at the doorway leading from the bathroom to the main motel room. He wore baggy trousers, an undershirt and bedroom slippers. A white towel was draped around his neck, and spots of shaving cream dotted his double chin.

"I'm Sanders," he confirmed. "Close the door and relax. The room's clean."

Sanders wasn't referring to the absence of dust. He meant that the room was clean of listening devices. Mervyn Sanders was a case officer for the National Security Agency, which is the largest American intelligence organization and the one that is least familiar to the general public.

"I assume you've been fully briefed?" Katz inquired.

"Yeah," Sanders said sourly as he crossed the room to gather up a small bottle of whiskey from a nightstand. "I was told you guys are real hotshots. Super commandos of some sort. Shoot-'em-up experts, right?"

"Smile when y'all say that, pawd-ner," McCarter declared in an exaggerated version of a 1930s Hollywood concept of a Texas drawl.

"Very funny," Sanders snorted, pouring himself a drink. "I heard about that big shoot-out at the airport this morning. About two dozen innocent people killed or injured. Oh, I know you guys figure you're big heroes because you gunned down the terrorists, right? Reports said a group of foreigners took out the bad guys. Not many details about who they were, but one report claimed one of the heroes was black. I suppose that was you, huh?"

The question had been directed at Calvin James. The hardass from Chicago opened his mouth in mock surprise and turned toward a wall mirror. His eyes opened wide with an exaggerated expression of astonishment.

"My God," James gasped. "You're right. I am black."

"Cute," Sanders muttered with disgust. "Have any of you cowboys ever heard of maintaining a low profile? How about security? Where the hell did they get you guys from? Extras in a Chuck Norris movie?"

"Mr. Sanders," Katz began quickly, before the razor-tongued McCarter or the sharp-witted James could speak. "The terrorists at the airport were something we hadn't planned on encountering, but it happened. They not only detonated an explosion in a crowded section of the airport, but they also machine-gunned civilians, police and airport security personnel. If we hadn't stopped them, the body count would have been much higher than it was. Don't expect us to apologize for what we did.''

"Justify it any way you want," Sanders replied. "To me you're nothing but a bunch of cowboys, and I think somebody in Washington has to be nuts to send you here...."

"I oughta put my boot up your arse, you silly sod," McCarter growled, his temper getting the better of him.

"Let me handle this," Katz told the Briton. He turned to Sanders, eyes as hard as marbles. "Let's get something straight, Sanders. Our authority comes from the Oval Office. That authority put us in charge, and you have been instructed by your superiors to take orders directly from us. We don't have time to listen to your petty complaints and whining. If you have any complaints about our methods, you can take that up with your control officer later. For now, you'll damn well follow orders."

"And if I don't," Sanders began, "what do you intend to do? Shoot me?"

"Anything's possible, mate," McCarter said with an unpleasant smile. The Briton pulled off his overcoat. The bulge of the Browning under his nubbly suit jacket was obvious.

"Let's change the subject," Calvin James suggested as he unbuttoned his coat and sat on the edge of the bed. "Tell us what the NSA has learned about the KGB which it has not shared with the SIA, CIA or the YMCA."

"Shit," Sanders muttered, gulping down his whiskey. "There's no proof the KGB is connected with the terrorist activity here in Finland."

"Department Eleven keeps a low profile," Katz commented as he fixed a Camel cigarette between two rigid fingers of his prosthetic hand and raised it to his lips.

"You know about Department Eleven?" Sanders raised his eyebrows. "I figured a hired gunslinger wouldn't need to bone up on KGB foreign operations."

"I probably read about it sometime when I was cleaning my six-shooter," Katz said dryly as he fired the cigarette with his Ronson lighter. "And if you don't start cooperating, your next assignment will be squatting in a half-frozen tent at a remote listening post in the worst tundra region that the NSA can find. If you don't think we can do it, make one more snotty remark, and we're out of here. By the end of the week you'll meet some penguins."

"Kinda cute birds in their little tuxedos," James added with an impish grin.

"Take it easy," Sanders said grimly. "Department Eleven generally operates within the Soviet embassy here in Helsinki. We try to keep tabs on them. So does the SIA and the CIA. Of course, since the business with the Democratic Liberation League started, the Company boys have been lying low at the U.S. embassy. Locals all figure the CIA is involved with the terrorists."

"That's why we contacted the NSA instead," Katz replied. "We figured you people would be able to operate more freely than the Company, considering the circumstances."

"Well, you were right," Sanders confirmed, pouring himself another drink. "Now, the top man with Department Eleven operations in Finland is Sergei Georgeovich Bajanov."

"The name is familiar," Katz said, knitting his brow. "Would that be Captain Bajanov, back in 1968? Soviet embassy in West Germany? BND thought he was connected with the beginnings of the Baader-Meinhof Gang, but there was never any real proof."

Sanders stared at Katz speechlessly. "How the hell did you know about that? You're right, of course, but Bajanov is a lieutenant colonel now. Big shot in the KGB. Oh, the Ivans have a decoy at the embassy. Phony Russky colonel who we're supposed to *believe* 's the real top spy, but Bajanov is the number one KGB pig in Finland."

"Very experienced agent," Katz remarked. "Is he in Helsinki?"

"Son of a bitch vanished about two weeks ago," Sanders answered. "Nobody knows where he is. One day we know his every move. We've got his office bugged, his movements followed, his telephones tapped. Then he gives us all the slip, and we don't have any idea where he got to."

"Bajanov probably knew every move your people made," McCarter said as he began to pace the floor. "Didn't it ever occur to you NSA blokes that it seemed *too easy* keeping tabs on a man with Bajanov's background?"

"That doesn't matter now," Katz told him. "Who were Bajanov's contacts in Helsinki? Finns, probably

young extremists, either left-wing or right-wing zealots. I doubt if Bajanov would have contacted any of
them personally. He'd probably have his agents do it,
or possibly cutouts who've been operating in Finland
for some time."

"Hell," Sanders said with a helpless shrug. "I don't
have information like that inside my head. I'll have to
check it out with the computers. That'll take time."

"The purpose of computers is to save time," James
remarked. "We need that information in a hurry."

"I can get it to you by tomorrow afternoon," Sanders declared. "Say five o'clock?"

"Five o'clock?" McCarter glared at the NSA agent.
"I thought you said you chaps used computers.
Sounds as if your filing system consists of notes
stuffed in old shoe boxes."

"I don't operate the computers myself," Sanders
answered, clearly annoyed by McCarter's attitude.
"But I'll get my people on it first thing in the morning."

"You'll get them on it now," Katz corrected. "The
United States and her allies are losing face, a lot of innocent people have been losing their lives, and the
nation of Finland is in danger of losing its freedom.
You and your people can lose one night's sleep to get
that information ready for us as soon as possible."

"Yes, sir," Sanders said through clenched teeth.
"You with Karista at his safe house? Pretty safe,
'cause even we don't know where it is."

"You know how intelligence operations work,"
Kalevi remarked as he took a notepad and pen from
his pocket. "We have to keep secrets...even from our
allies. I'll write down a number so you can call me

when you have what we need. I'll pick you up and take you wherever Karista decides we should meet. Agreed?''

"Sure," Sanders answered, clearly disgusted with all four of his guests.

"Thank you for your time, Mr. Sanders," Katz told the NSA agent. "We'd better be going. Two of our partners are checking on a possible lead outside of Helsinki. They should be returning in another hour or two."

**8**

"Come on, Rolf," Rafael Encizo rasped as he un-buckled Lautanen's safety belt. "Help me, damn it!"

"Uh," the Finnish agent groaned, massaging his neck with one hand as he started to rise from his seat. "What happened?"

"We're going to burn to death if we don't get the hell out of here!" Encizo replied, pulling the dazed SIA man into the aisle.

The fire had moved across the sabotaged wing of the wrecked Beech airplane and spread to the carriage of the craft. The heat had helped revive Encizo as he had begun to lose consciousness. When he had opened his eyes to see a wall of flame at the window, the Cuban's senses had returned dramatically—especially his sense of survival. Encizo unstrapped himself from his seat and hurried to Rolf Lautanen. The Finn had been dazed by the impact of the crash, but he didn't appear to be injured. Encizo wasn't sure what sort of shape Gary Manning was in. The Canadian lay motionless on the floor of the aircraft.

Lautanen was moaning as he rubbed his neck. He allowed Encizo to haul him to his feet. "I remember..."

"Help me with Gary!" Encizo ordered, pulling Lautanen to where Manning lay. "Hurry up, or we'll find out what it was like to be inside the ovens at Dachau!"

"What about Sven?" Lautanen asked, recalling the pilot.

"He's dead," Encizo replied as he grabbed one of Manning's arms and braced it across his neck and shoulders.

Lautanen grabbed the other arm, and they hauled Manning up from the floor. Fortunately, an emergency hatch to the plane had broken off when the plane crashed. They carried Manning to the exit to lower him outside. Encizo noticed a scarlet ribbon of blood on Manning's left cheek.

When the unconscious Canadian was placed on top of the snow, they climbed from the plane. The flames continued to grow, licking the flank of the wrecked plane. Encizo and Lautanen gathered up Manning and waded through the knee-deep snow, attempting to run from the burning Beech. The snow bogged down their progress. They felt as if they were wearing cement boots, and their muscles ached from the strain of Manning's weight.

Lautanen lost his footing and fell forward into the snow. He pulled down Manning and yanked Encizo off balance. The Cuban struggled to stay on his feet, but the world seemed to transfer into a whirling blur. The bright blaze of the flaming plane glared from the jumbled collection of his fragmented vision. Encizo half turned and landed face first in the snow.

The fire reached the fuel tank. The plane exploded with a monstrous roar. The three men sank deeper into the snow, hugging the frozen ground as burning debris showered the area. Chunks of hot metal fell near Encizo, and snow hissed less than a foot from the Cuban's left ear as a burning missile slid into the dense white carpet.

Lautanen cried out and twitched wildly, then rolled onto his back and dragged his right leg through the snow. Encizo crawled over to help the SIA agent. Lautanen's features were contorted with pain, his eyes tightly closed and his mouth drawn taut across clenched teeth.

"My leg..." Lautanen groaned as he reached for his thigh with gloved hands. "Feels like I have been shot..."

"Let me look," Encizo urged. He helped Lautanen roll over on his side. "Oh, Christ."

A burning chunk of plastic and cast aluminum had struck Lautanen in the back of his right thigh. The hot projectile had scorched through the Finn's trousers and burned into his flesh. Encizo gripped the metal with gloved fingers.

"This is gonna hurt," he warned.

"It hurts *now*," Lautanen rasped. "Go ahead."

Encizo yanked the shard from the Finn's thigh. Skin tore and blood bubbled. Lautanen uttered a choked cry and fainted. Encizo gripped an artery under the Finn's buttocks to try to reduce the bleeding. He fumbled with the buttons of his parka with his other hand.

"Goddamn it," the Cuban croaked. "Why didn't I bring a first-aid kit? This is the sort of thing Calvin should be here to deal with...."

But Calvin James wasn't present, and Encizo knew he would have to handle the crisis alone. He rapidly reviewed what he had in his pockets that might serve as an improvised bandage. No handkerchief, he thought. No gauze, not even a Band-Aid.

Encizo reached inside his coat and grabbed a shirt pocket. He pulled hard and tore it from his shirt. The Cuban placed the patch of cloth over Lautanen's wound, then reached inside the parka to seize the other shirt pocket. Blood began to seep into the improvised bandage as Encizo released the pressure he'd maintained on Lautanen's artery. He was vaguely aware of loose articles sliding under his parka, articles that fell free when he ripped off the pockets of his shirt.

"Keep your head," Encizo muttered to himself. "You've gotta keep your head."

He placed the second pocket over the first to reinforce the bandage. Encizo applied pressure to the wounded Finn's artery with one hand as he drew his Heckler & Koch autoloader from the shoulder holster under his left arm. He tucked the pistol in his belt and reached for the hilt of the Tanto Cold Steel knife on his hip.

The Cuban drew the fighting blade from its leather sheath. Six inches of flawless high-quality steel gleamed with reflected starlight. Encizo carefully slid the Tanto inside his parka and slipped the razor edge under the strap to the holster. The Cold Steel blade easily sawed through the leather. He switched the knife to his other hand and cut the strap to the holster rig at his right shoulder.

Encizo pulled the severed pieces of leather from under his parka and cut the sections into roughly equal parts. He tied a strap around Lautanen's thigh to hold the bandage in place and wound another strap three inches higher to apply pressure to the artery.

"Tourniquet," Encizo thought out loud. "I need a stick or something...."

He glanced around and discovered that part of a metal rib from the wing of the plane had landed less than a yard away. Encizo was thankful for this small offering and gathered it up. He placed it on the tourniquet bandage and wrapped the ends of the strap around the metal bar. Encizo twisted the rod to tighten the cord and tied it into place.

"Gary?" Encizo called to Manning, aware that his partner hadn't stirred. "Gary, can you hear me?"

The Canadian lay motionless, facedown in the snow. Encizo left Rolf Lautanen and hurried to Manning's side, then rolled him onto his back. The blood on Manning's face formed a long red streak. The Canadian's eyes were closed, his lips slightly parted. Encizo placed two fingers at the side of Manning's neck to check for a pulse at the carotid artery.

"If I can't find one, I'll have to try CPR," the Cuban said to himself, trying to build up hope that the situation wasn't as desperate as it would seem if he took the time to fully consider it.

"No," Manning moaned softly and opened his eyes to stare up at Encizo. "You're not my type."

*"Muchas gracis, Dios,"* Encizo declared with relief, rolling his eyes toward heaven. He wasn't a particularly religious man, but discovering that his friend was still alive encouraged the belief that God occasionally took a hand in the events of men.

Manning started to sit up, uttered a harsh cough and rolled onto his side to vomit into the snow. Clutching his left forearm, he hissed with pain, then slowly turned his head and stared up at his partner.

"Last I recall we were inside a plane," he remarked, glancing at the burning wreckage. "Is that what's left of it?"

"That's right," Encizo confirmed. "You, Rolf and I got out alive. The pilot didn't make it. The canopy at the nose of the plane was literally crushed by the crash, and I'm sure Sven was killed instantly."

"I'd be dead, too, if you and Rolf hadn't saved me," Manning said, gingerly sliding his left forearm inside his parka. "Thanks, amigo."

"That's what friends are for," Encizo replied. "Rolf was hit by flying shrapnel when the plane exploded. I don't know if he'll be able to walk, and I think he might have suffered whiplash to his neck during the crash. How do you feel?"

"My head feels like somebody worked it over with a jackhammer," Manning answered, trying to take slow, deep breaths as he spoke. "And my left arm is broken."

"Shit," Encizo said with a sigh. "You sure?"

"Oh, yeah," Manning assured him. "Hurts like a bitch. Where the hell are we, anyway?"

"I guess this is Lappi," the Cuban replied.

He had been too busy to pay much attention to the environment and had noticed little except the deep snow and the bitter cold, which was severe enough to convince him not to remove his parka in order to strip off the shoulder holster. Encizo scanned the area. It resembled a desert of snow with a few spruce trees.

The fire from the burning remnants of the plane were dying, smothered by the snow.

Flames licked the trunk of a spruce tree, but the fire didn't spread. The tree was too green to burn easily, and water dripped on the blaze from melting snow on the lower branches. The fire didn't have a chance. Very little seemed able to survive in the bleak region.

"Any suggestions about what we should do now?" Encizo asked Manning. "You're from Canada. You said you went on hunting trips in this kind of weather."

"Yeah," Manning replied as he slowly sat up. "But that was with a nice log cabin to stay in after the sun came down. That included a fireplace, sleeping bags and warm blankets."

"Great," the Cuban muttered. "Well, I don't think we can cut down these trees and build a cabin. I'm not even sure we can keep a fire going."

"We can't stay here squatting in the snow and shivering," Manning began. He grunted and touched his right hand to the gash above his left eyebrow. "God, I wish I had a bottle of aspirin or maybe a dose of morphine."

"I wish we had a radio so we could contact somebody to rescue us," Encizo remarked. "I don't think Sven had a chance to call in a Mayday before the plane went down, and the crash sure wiped out the radio."

"I don't suppose you managed to salvage our supplies in those backpacks?" Manning inquired.

"Are you kidding?" Encizo said crossly. "I was still only half-conscious when I got you and Rolf out of the plane. I was too groggy to think about anything else."

"Okay," Manning assured him. "I just asked. We had some stuff packed in there that would be nice to have now. Too late to change what's already happened. We just have to improvise—"

A long howl interrupted Manning, followed by a response like a lonely siren cry. More howls joined the choir echoing above the moaning wind. Encizo pulled the H&K pistol from his belt.

"Did you hear that?" the Cuban asked.

"Just some wolves," Manning told him. "Karista mentioned there were some packs still roaming Lappi. No big deal."

"Wolves?" Encizo replied, glaring at Manning. "There are goddamn wolves around here, and you expect me to relax?"

"Stories about wolves attacking people are bullshit," Manning snorted, annoyed with Encizo's attitude. "There are wolves in the United States and Canada, but I never heard of a single verified incident of wolves attacking human beings in either country. A rabid wolf, maybe. If we had a dog, the wolves might rush us to get to Rover, but they won't attack people."

"I remember hearing that hammerhead sharks wouldn't attack people, either," Encizo muttered.

"Look," Manning began with exasperation. "I've encountered wolf packs in Canada. If any wolves show up, just fire a shot in the air, and they'll take off for the hills. Wolves are very shy and easily startled. Believe me, wolves are the least of our problems."

"I hope you know what you're talking about," Encizo said with a sigh as he put the pistol back in his belt. "I'm gonna inspect the wreckage from the plane and see what can be salvaged. Can you look after Rolf?''

"Right now I can barely look after myself," Manning confessed. "Don't worry—we'll be okay."

"I don't feel okay," Lautanen commented with a groan as he propped himself up on an elbow. "But at least I'm awake now. Feels like you patched up my leg."

"Not very well, I'm afraid. But it ought to do until we get out of here. You two just relax for now," Encizo replied, then unloosed the tourniquet on the Finn's leg to maintain circulation.

"We can't relax too much," Manning declared as he slowly got to his feet, trying to protect his broken left arm as he rose. "If you don't move around in cold weather, you can get frostbite. A bad case of frostbite can result in gangrene, and these conditions are ideal for getting frostbite. Temperature is at freezing level, windchill factor makes it worse, and we're all damp, as well. We gotta keep our blood circulating, or there's a good chance we'll wind up losing some fingers and toes—or worse. I've seen victims of severe frostbite who had to have an entire limb amputated due to advanced gangrene."

"That's what I like about you, Gary," Encizo snorted as he headed toward the wreckage. "You're always so blasted cheerful."

"I'm just stating some facts," Manning insisted. "Not facts I really want to think about, either. After all, I've got a broken arm, and I can't move the fingers of my left hand. That means my odds of getting frostbite are a lot higher than yours. Situation isn't gonna change because we choose to ignore it."

"I'm probably going to lose this leg," Lautanen said grimly. "Aren't I?"

"We're going to get through this mess," Encizo declared, examining the twisted metal and charred debris of the destroyed aircraft and hoping he sounded more confident than he felt.

## 9

"Have you seen the morning paper, Major?" Lieutenant Colonel Bajanov inquired as Anatoliy Kharkov entered the KGB control officer's secret headquarters at Kotka. "I'm certain they will read the feature story in Moscow."

"The incident at the airport was very unfortunate," Kharkov said with a grim nod. "But I have warned you about these young zealots. They're unstable, mentally unbalanced and totally unpredictable."

"We are trying to create a state of political chaos in Finland," Bajanov declared as he angrily swept through the storage section of the warehouse to the office. "That doesn't mean we want senseless bloodbaths with extraordinary body counts."

"What do you expect from terrorists?" Kharkov asked with a shrug. "That's what these damn fanatics are. They can call themselves patriots or urban guerrillas if they wish, but they are simply destructive individuals who get carried away with the emotional thrill of slaughtering human life."

"Very strange criticism from a man who is himself a professional assassin," Bajanov said dryly, stomping across the floor of his office to the desk.

"The difference is the fact I *am* a professional," Kharkov replied, taking the verbal barb without any evidence of resentment. "Blaming me won't solve any problems, Comrade Colonel. You've been giving me my orders. Half the people I've been in touch with are contacts you made in Finland long before I was assigned to this mission. The fault is not mine, Comrade. The incident at the airport was simply a foul-up by a group of young fanatics who were trying to impress their fellow young fanatics and show off their ability to butcher large numbers of people at one time. I suspect they wanted to show how they could gun down armed police officers and security personnel. Killing an armed opponent is pretty brave for a terrorist. Most of the time they just toss their bombs and run."

"That's all they were supposed to do at the airport," Bajanov insisted. "If they had simply planted the bomb and left, the explosion would have killed a handful of people to create terror and would have still gained the desired publicity. Instead, those fools started shooting their automatic weapons. They killed a few more people and got themselves dead in the process."

"At least we don't have to worry if they're going to talk to the authorities," Kharkov remarked, taking his cigarette case from a pocket. "Frankly, I don't see how this will endanger our mission here. The six idiots are dead. Even if they were alive, they wouldn't be able to tell anyone anything of value, because they didn't know anything to tell. When the police and the SIA check into the background of those morons, they'll discover all six were associated with a neofascist group which supported NATO and opposed communism.''

''They were killed by a group of foreigners,'' Bajanov commented. ''Strangers from either Western Europe or America. Apparently they were only armed with pistols, but they had little trouble taking out six gunmen armed with automatic weapons.''

''Professionals against amateurs,'' Kharkov said with a mirthless smile. ''An automatic weapon simply fires more ammunition faster than conventional firearms. That's not enough to even the odds when the opponents have more skill and experience. The terrorists at the airport didn't have a chance against real professionals.''

''Foreigners,'' Bajanov repeated. ''Special team from the American CIA? British SIS?''

''I don't think so,'' Kharkov replied thoughtfully. ''Not really their style. They're probably combat veterans. Maybe some sort of new NATO antiterrorist squad. An international version of the SAS or GSG-9. Or it could be that strike team working for the Americans. The one everyone in the KGB has heard rumors about but the Kremlin doesn't want to talk about.''

''I've heard those rumors,'' Bajanov said grimly. ''Supposedly the same group defeated Kostov in Greece and Yousopov in India. There was even a story that the KGB, GRU and a hundred of our best Soviet paratroopers conducted a seek-and-destroy mission in the United States to assassinate that group. None of them ever returned to the Soviet Union.''

''Probably exaggerations,'' Kharkov commented, blowing a smoke ring toward the ceiling. ''At any rate, it would be an additional victory for our operation if we took care of those bastards. Moscow would certainly be pleased. . . ."

"No," Bajanov said sharply. "That isn't part of our mission, and seeking a confrontation with them will endanger the success of our operation here. I don't want you to take any action against them, Major. Agreed?"

"You're in command, Comrade General," Kharkov said with a sigh. "But as an assassin I find the challenge most compelling. Most of my targets are helpless sheep. Killing them is rather like butchering pigs in a slaughterhouse. Very easy and very dull. Now, killing a group of professionals, that would be an exciting change of pace, eh?"

"I said no, Comrade," Bajanov insisted, opening a desk drawer to remove a single sheet of paper. "I have something else for you to do. A minor cutout operative named Taivas has been working for us for about a year now. He was an agent in place at a small airstrip where he was supposed to keep tabs on a pilot occasionally hired by the SIA for courier jobs. Last night, Taivas decided to take some direct action on his own without authorization."

"Did he cause a problem?" Kharkov inquired.

"Perhaps," Bajanov replied. "The pilot and three passengers left the airfield to head for Lappi. Taivas claims he heard them speaking English, so he assumed they were CIA, and he sabotaged the plane. The aircraft didn't return, so Taivas is quite happy with himself and convinced his efforts were successful."

"Perhaps they were," Kharkov said with a smile. "I suppose Comrade Taivas expects to be rewarded for his heroic deed?"

"Here's his address, phone number and usual places where contacts are made," Bajanov explained, handing the paper to Kharkov. "I want you to meet with Taivas and reward him for his enthusiasm."

"Taivas lives in Vantaa," Kharkov mused, reading the information carefully and committing it to memory. "Olav used to live in that city. I'm certain he can find this address."

"Take care of it as soon as possible," Bajanov ordered.

"I'm on my way, Comrade Colonel," the assassin replied with a grin as he returned the paper to Bajanov.

The KGB colonel nodded with approval and snapped open a cigarette lighter. He struck the wheel to spark flame to life and set the paper ablaze. The fire burned the sheet as Bajanov held the blackened paper over the rim of a metal ashtray. Kharkov left the office while his commander finished destroying the message.

MAUNO TAIVAS HUMMED CHEERFULLY as he strolled along the sidewalk toward his apartment building. He carried a sack of groceries, including a bottle of vodka, Danish cheese and Russian caviar. Taivas planned to celebrate. He had shown the KGB that he could be counted on to do more than simply spy on government lackeys and acquire bits and pieces of minor information. Soon he would be promoted to a position of greater importance within the revolutionary movement.

A stranger dressed in a long trench coat and fur hat sat on a bench at a bus stop, glancing through a newspaper without reading it. He smiled thinly as he saw Taivas walk home from the shops. Kharkov recognized Taivas from the data sheet Bajanov had shown him—the same sheet the colonel had burned. Kharkov folded his newspaper and placed it on the bench as Taivas approached.

Kharkov rose from the bench to greet the mechanic. "Beautiful day, isn't it?"

A blanket of snow covered the cobblestone streets, and an icy wind whipped down from the north, but Taivas suspected the stranger wasn't referring to the weather.

"It is a nice day," he replied with a nod. "Have we met before?"

"We have mutual friends, Comrade," Kharkov said, glancing about with exaggerated caution. In fact, he had already made certain no one was close enough to hear their conversation. "I am Major Kharkov, KGB. We have to talk, Comrade."

"Of course," Taivas said eagerly.

"It concerns your trip to Moscow," Kharkov whispered. "We can't discuss this here. Follow me."

"Moscow?" Taivas asked in astonishment.

"Not here?" Kharkov muttered softly. "Come with me."

Taivas dutifully followed Kharkov across the street. The Soviet agent led him into an alley. A truck was parked there, with Olav, the big henchman with the dense red beard, sitting behind the steering wheel. He calmly started the engine as Kharkov escorted Taivas to the rear of the vehicle.

"Get in," the Russian instructed, gesturing at the tailgate of the truck.

"I'm not sure..." Taivas began with apprehension. He noticed Larrs waiting for him inside the back of the truck. The bearded blond smiled and nodded at Taivas, but there was something unpleasant about the big man's expression.

"I said get in," Kharkov insisted. His gloved fist closed around the Walther pistol in his coat pocket. He jammed the muzzle against Taivas's spine. "Do it!"

Taivas reluctantly stepped onto the tailgate. Larrs seized the smaller man's arms and easily hauled him into the back of the truck. Taivas gasped with fear and surprise. Larrs rammed a big knee into his groin. The bag of groceries fell to the floor of the truck as Taivas doubled up with a choking groan. Larrs hit him in the nape of the neck, knocking him to the floor.

Kharkov gestured toward the front of the truck. Olav saw the motion in the rearview mirror and shifted gears as Kharkov climbed into the back with Larrs and Taivas. The truck slowly rolled forward from the mouth of the alley. Kharkov pulled down the tarp to conceal the activities in the rear of the vehicle from outsiders.

Larrs had pinned Taivas with a knee at the small of his back. The big blonde handcuffed Taivas and tied a gag in place around his mouth. Larrs then drew a large knife from a sheath under his coat and held the twelve-inch blade in front of Taivas's face to make certain the prisoner got a good look at the weapon.

Taivas recognized the knife. It was a scramasax, a modern version of the traditional fighting knife of the sixth century. The scramasax resembled an American bowie knife, with a heavy single-edged blade. Larrs held the edge close to Taivas's neck as Kharkov sat on the floor next to them.

"You poor little amateur," the KGB killer said with mock sympathy. "You really thought we'd be grateful because you sabotaged that plane? All you accomplished by your rash actions was to alert our enemies that they were on the right track. We're supposed to thank you for that?"

Taivas rolled his eyes to gaze up at Kharkov, muttering something through his gag, but the words were unintelligible.

"Perhaps those men were CIA or something like CIA," Kharkov continued. "So you killed them. So what did that accomplish? There are always others to take the place of enemies you kill. The CIA, SIS or whatever outfit is involved will certainly conduct an investigation now. It won't take them long to realize you were probably responsible. They'd make you talk. It wouldn't be hard to break you, and you'd tell them everything you know. We can't allow that, Taivas. When you sabotaged that plane, you signed your own death warrant in the process."

The truck bounced over a crack in the street, but it didn't stop. The vehicle traveled at a slow, easy pace toward the city limits. Kharkov had chosen the site for Taivas's grave. The body would be weighted down with rocks and deposited in a half-frozen lake. Taivas's corpse probably would be found eventually, but it was unlikely to be discovered before spring.

"What have you brought us, Taivas?" Kharkov inquired as he examined the contents of the groceries. "Vodka, bread, cheese, caviar. How very kind of you. My associates and I appreciate these gifts. Perhaps we'll have a little feast later. We'll be certain to drink a toast to you, Comrade."

Kharkov chuckled with amusement as the truck headed for the open roads beyond the boundaries of Vantaa.

## 10

Rafael Encizo, Gary Manning and Rolf Lautanen sat huddled together against the trunk of the largest spruce tree. They were surrounded by branches cut from the few trees in the area. Encizo was exhausted from the task. He had climbed three different trees and hacked off more than a dozen branches of various sizes, using only his Cold Steel Tanto knife as a tool. Fortunately, the thick blade was very sturdy, but the chore had been quite demanding of both the knife and its owner.

The three men had constructed a crude hut with the branches. They had set several branches on the ground at the base of the tree to form a dense carpet of soft evergreen before building walls around it. Encizo had to do most of the work, because Manning could only use one arm and Lautanen could barely stand, even with the assistance of a stripped-down tree limb for a crutch.

The hut was flimsy, but the thin walls of evergreen branches reduced the force of the howling wind. The interior was heated only by the body warmth of the three men. The flexible walls were reinforced by metal ribs from the plane wreckage, and the carpet of branches protected them from the damp, snow-packed

A loud snarl cut off Manning's remark as a branch was abruptly plucked from the hut. Encizo glimpsed the dark snout of a wolf, whose long white teeth were clamped around the branch. A yellow eye with a large iris stared in through the gap in the wall. A gray paw burst through another section of the hut. Claws raked Manning's upper left arm, tearing the parka sleeve, and he groaned as fresh pain jolted along his broken forearm.

At least two wolves were attacking their shelter. One beast thrust its shaggy head through the flimsy barrier, its pointed ears flattened against its spade-shaped skull, its jaws parted to reveal daggerlike fangs. Another beast tore at the hut with powerful teeth, dislodging branches from the makeshift dwelling.

Encizo pulled the H&K pistol from his belt. Manning reached for his Walther P-5, but Lautanen recoiled from the snapping jaws of a canine invader and fell against the Canadian before Manning could draw his weapon. Encizo tried to aim the Heckler & Koch at the wolf's head as the beast shoved its thick shoulders through the wall of the hut.

He thumbed off the safety catch and squeezed the trigger. The H&K roared and recoiled in Encizo's fist. The wolf yelped with pain as a 9 mm slug tore into the side of its neck. The beast raised its head, and Encizo placed a shot under the jaw. The second bullet powered upward to pierce the animal's cranium. It collapsed, knocking over a large portion of the hut. The wolf twitched once and snapped its jaws near Lautanen's right foot. The Finn kicked out with his left foot, but the beast was dead before his boot struck its bullet-punctured skull.

The second wolf retreated from the assault, startled by the gunshots. As Manning drew his Walther pistol, he lurched against a wall of the hut. The interwoven branches gave way under his weight, and he tumbled on his back into the snow. The exposed Canadian fired two shots into the sky as fast as he could trigger the double-action autoloader.

Encizo pushed aside a large portion of the shelter and swung his H&K pistol toward the wreckage of the Beech aircraft. The wolves bounded away, except for one beast that stood its ground, head lowered and teeth bared in a fierce posture. The animal was big, nearly six feet long and well muscled, its eyes glowing. The dark fur appeared black in the shadows as Encizo aimed his pistol at the defiant wolf.

The animal sensed danger and bolted an instant before Encizo triggered his weapon. A parabellum slug kicked up a cloud of snow near the wolf's hind legs as it raced after the pack. The creatures howled as they ran, but none turned back to confront the men armed with the loud noisemakers.

"Jesus," Manning said breathlessly, climbing to his knees in the snow. "Those wolves actually attacked us!"

"No shit," Encizo snorted, scanning the area to make certain all the predators had fled. "You wanna give me another lecture about how harmless wolves are, or don't you want your other arm broken?"

"I just can't believe it," Manning remarked, glancing down at the body of the slain wolf. "I've seen wolves in Canada lots of times. They never acted like this."

"You'd better believe it!" Encizo said crossly. "They huffed and puffed and blew our stick house down and damn near had us for breakfast."

"This animal doesn't have rabies," Manning remarked, examining the wolf's gaping jaws. "This just doesn't make sense. I never heard of wolves really attacking people before."

"That's because you aren't a European," Lautanen stated, struggling with his improvised crutch to rise to his feet.

"I know there were legends about killer wolves in Europe," Manning replied. "But that was because of epidemics of rabies, wasn't it? Sick, mad wolves. That's where the werewolf legend came from."

"Not entirely," Lautanen insisted. "Look around. See how barren this place is? How much food do you think these wolves can find here? They've been desperate for some time, and they've learned to overcome their fear of man because they discovered human flesh as a new addition to their diet."

"The half-eaten bodies that were discovered out here by the trappers..." Encizo commented. "I've heard that lions and tigers can develop a taste for human flesh and turn into man-eaters. I always figured that was bullshit."

"I don't know about that," Lautanen answered. "But I know wolves in Europe have attacked and eaten people in the past. I'm not talking about legends or werewolves or anything of that sort. I'm talking about *fact*."

"But wolves in Europe aren't any different from wolves in the United States or Canada," Manning remarked, staring down at the slain beast. "This sucker looks just like a timber wolf you might find in North America.''

"The history of America is different from that of Europe,'' Lautanen insisted. "The American Indians were skilled woodsmen and hunters, while European peasants usually were superstitious and frightened by nature and darkness. Hunting and fighting was done by professionals or by village men chosen for the task, and wolves weren't as quick to learn fear of men in Europe. But there were wars in Europe, and plagues that killed thousands. The bodies of the dead were often left on the battlefields in those days, and victims of disease were often dumped into shallow communal graves.''

"And occasionally they served as dinner for wolves,'' Encizo said with a nod.

"Exactly,'' Lautanen confirmed. "Wolves may be predators, but they also scavenge. When they were starving during harsh winters and found fresh supplies of human flesh, they consumed it as they would the meat of any other dead creature they happened upon. Stories of wolf attacks were especially common in France, where many battles were fought and many bodies left on the ground afterward. Especially during times of plague, when it was impossible to keep up with burying the dead, they were frequently dumped into garbage pits outside the city of Paris. Wolves often rummaged through the garbage....''

"And you think we've got a similar situation here?'' Manning asked. "Terrorists or the KGB or whoever murdered the diplomats brought their bodies here. Half-starved wolves found the corpses, and now they realize people can provide them with occasional meals.''

"It has happened before," Lautanen replied. "Not too surprising, really. Reindeer are still being bred in captivity, but the wild reindeer are dying out. We Finns have been using up our forests. Wood products, paper, wood pulp are our nation's major export. The trees are becoming more scarce; the forests are becoming bare. The reindeer and other animal life have suffered, and the wolves must now survive on whatever they can find."

"Well, they found us," Encizo said grimly. "At least they still seem to fear gunshots, even if they aren't afraid of us. I've got six rounds left in this magazine and one spare mag with nine rounds. How about you guys?"

"Six rounds and a spare mag with eight rounds," Manning answered. "Didn't you bring your Walther PPK for backup?"

"No," Encizo said with a sigh. "I didn't."

"You *always* carry that gun...." Manning began.

"Well, I didn't this time, damn it," Encizo snapped. "I usually carry at least two spare mags for each weapon, too, but I didn't figure we were going to wind up stranded out here with the White Fang family. What have you got, Rolf?"

"Nothing," Lautanen said sheepishly. "I didn't think I'd need a gun."

"Great," Encizo muttered with disgust. "So we've got two guns and twenty-nine rounds total. I wonder how many wolves are out there."

"Maybe they won't try us again," Manning suggested.

"You're the guy who told me not to worry about them in the first place," Encizo muttered.

"What the hell do you want from me, Rafael?" the Canadian demanded. "An apology? Okay, I'm sorry. I based my opinion on my experience in the past, and I screwed up. Does that make you happy?"

"I'm the one who should apologize," Encizo said gently. "My temper is a little frayed right now. I don't know why, exactly. The cold and the snow. This isn't what I'm used to. Then those goddamn wolves scared the hell out of me. Men with guns or knives I can handle. Even sharks don't scare me too badly, but these wolves are sort of like sharks on dry land. Like some sort of childhood nightmare that's really happening now. The fact that it's still night although my watch says it's nine o'clock in the morning doesn't make matters any easier. I feel like I've found myself on another planet, and nothing is familiar."

"This is a pretty rough experience for all of us," Manning assured him. "Rolf and I are sort of busted up, so we can't help you much, and you have to take on most of the work. I know it's tough."

"Hell, we've been through worse," Encizo said with a smile, although he couldn't think of an incident that had seemed bleaker—except when he had been a prisoner in Cuba. "We'll get out of this."

"Rolf," Manning began. "Do you know if there are any towns around here?"

"Not very close, I'm afraid," Lautanen replied. "Maybe three hundred kilometers southeast of where we are. Bear in mind that I'm not sure where we are myself."

"That's a long way in this sort of weather," Manning commented. "If we make a litter for Rolf, we might be able to make about thirty kilometers a day if we push it."

"You could cover twice that distance if you went on without me," Lautanen told him.

"We're not gonna do that," Encizo declared. "Nobody gets left behind. In fact, I don't think we should try to leave. All I see out there is more snow. No trees. No hills. No shelter from this goddamn cold."

"Well," Manning said as he glanced down at the dead wolf. "We've got something we didn't have before. An extra fur coat. Can I borrow your knife, Rafael?"

"You gonna skin it?" Encizo asked, surprised.

"Why not?" the Canadian replied. "The wolf doesn't need the fur anymore. It has a thick winter coat, too. It'll make a nice warm blanket."

"My Tanto knife is getting sort of dull," Encizo commented as he reached down to draw a Gerber Mark I fighting dagger from a boot sheath. "You might have to use this blade to start cutting."

"Probably need both knives," Manning confirmed, kneeling beside the dead animal. "I've skinned and butchered deer plenty of times before. This shouldn't be much different. By the way, is anybody else hungry?"

"You're not serious?" Lautanen grimaced. "You don't intend to eat a wolf...."

"You see anything else to eat around here?" the Canadian inquired, taking the Gerber knife from Encizo. "I don't know how long we'll be stuck out here, but we'll need our strength, and we're not gonna get much energy from eating snow.''

"Still,'' Encizo agreed with Lautanen. "Eating a wolf . . .''

"Hey, look at it this way,'' Manning insisted. "This wolf would have eaten *us*.''

## 11

"Still no news about your friends," Orm Karista announced as Yakov Katzenelenbogen, Calvin James and David McCarter entered his office. "There has been no radio contact with the plane since last night. The pilot did report that they were over Lappi, but no one is quite sure where."

"Something must have happened," Katz said grimly. "The pilot didn't call in a Mayday."

"No," Karista replied, shaking his head. "Apparently the plane either crashed somewhere in the Lappi province or...or it exploded in midair."

"We've got to find them," James said, turning toward Katz. "They could be out there, stranded and possibly hurt. Can't just leave 'em, man."

"Sanders came up with some information we have to look into," Katz told him. "Mr. Karista? When will you send planes or helicopters to search the area?"

"Weather conditions are very bad right now," the Finnish case officer explained. "Difficult to get pilots willing to go up until the snow lets up a bit."

"I'm a bloody pilot," McCarter announced. "I'll go up in any damn thing you can get me. Plane, helicopter or a blasted weather balloon with a basket attached."

"No," Katz said firmly. "We're short two men as it is. We can't afford to lose you, too."

"Damn it, Y—" McCarter began, but he remembered to call Katz by his cover name. "You can't just scratch them off, Goldberg."

"You know me well enough to know I care very much about my men," Katz insisted. "You also know we have a mission to carry out, and the success of that mission is more important than any of us as individuals. Sanchez and Jennings understand this, too, and I think they'd approve of my decision."

"Yeah," James agreed reluctantly. "I guess you're right."

"We will send a search party as soon as possible," Karista promised. "I'm sorry there's not much we can do right now."

"I'm sure you'll do what you can," McCarter said with a sigh. "For now we'd better concentrate on that Valkonnie bloke, or whatever the hell his name is."

"Who?" Karista asked with a frown.

"Valkeinen," Katz explained. "Erik Valkeinen. Our NSA connection, Mr. Sanders, came up with that name. Valkeinen is the ringleader of a militant group of Marxists. A radical bunch which has been officially condemned by the Finnish Communist Party. Maybe you've heard of them. The Red War Ring?"

"Unfortunately," Karista said with a sigh. "The Punainen SotaSormus, or the PSS. We had some trouble with them back in the seventies. Sort of a minor league Baader-Meinhof Gang that never got too far. The members wear a solid red ring on the left hand. Same as a wedding ring. Symbolic of being married to the cause of the Red revolution."

"How touching," McCarter said dryly. "Seems to me that would be something of a 'red giveaway.' Those blokes would be fairly easy to spot."

"Not as easy as you might think," Karista corrected. "There's no law against wearing a red ring, and some people wear them who have no connection with any sort of extremist politics. However, when the PSS started throwing bombs and assaulting police officers, the majority of the members were rounded up and arrested. We'd thought that was the end of that nasty little band. I don't think the leader was ever apprehended. How did the NSA find out about this Valkeinen character?"

"Sanders didn't say," Katz replied. "The NSA never tells anyone anything without a reason. We had to threaten Sanders to get him to give us anything at all."

"Perhaps I should threaten him, as well," Karista said sourly. "The NSA is probably keeping other secrets from my organization, secrets that concern the national security of Finland. Why the hell didn't he tell us about Valkeinen before? We're all on the same side, aren't we?"

"Intelligence networks never share any information freely," Katz said with a shrug. "How much data has the SIA shared with American intelligence outfits or with other West European intel groups?"

"We occasionally trade information," Karista said carefully. "But I suppose we never give away anything unless we want something in return. You know, I can't help being very curious about you people. You seem to be able to cut through all the bureaucracy that bogs down intelligence work and get uncooperative organizations to work together. How do you do it?''

"That's one secret we can't share with you," Katz said with a thin smile. "However, I can tell you some details about Valkeinen and the Red War Ring."

"That will please me enough to lose my curiosity about who you men are and how you operate," the Finn assured him.

"According to the NSA," Katz began, lighting a Camel cigarette and holding it between two metal hooks at the end of his right arm. This prosthesis was his favorite, because it functioned much the same as a real hand and allowed him to do far more than the five-fingered device he had worn before. "Valkeinen was in touch with Lieutenant Colonel Bajanov."

"KGB, right?" Karista rolled his eyes toward the ceiling. "The NSA knew about a field-grade KGB officer running around Finland, and they didn't bother to share that with us, either...."

"You want to hear about this or not?" James inquired.

"Bajanov vanished some months ago," Katz explained. "That is to say, NSA lost track of him. My guess is he's still in Finland, but probably not in Helsinki. However, Sanders did tell us that Valkeinen and several other members of the Red War Ring recently moved into apartments near the Market Square here in Helsinki. Apparently they found some low-rent housing in the area, which I understand is a pretty good trick."

"The Kauppatori District," Karista said with a nod. "It's located near the South Harbor. Very desirable area for businesses of all sorts. It also tends to be very crowded there. I hope you aren't planning to stage a gun battle there."

"We don't want that to happen any more than you do," Katz assured him. "But Valkeinen is too valuable to let him slip away. Most of the terrorists involved in this business probably have no idea the KGB is pulling the strings. Valkeinen not only knows the Soviets are the real masterminds, he probably knows where we can find the control agents who are manipulating the terrorists."

"You know those turkeys at the airport turned out to be members of a right-wing outfit opposed to communism," James added. "If we can prove the KGB is behind this mess, all the right-wing nuts involved will drop out quicker than a high school kid with a winning lottery ticket. Hell, they might even turn on their control officers like overtrained attack dogs."

"I see," Karista said with a nod. "Valkeinen could be the key to turning this whole mess around. How many men will we need?"

"The ideal situation for a raid is to outnumber your opponents as much as possible," McCarter commented, lighting up a Player's. "But there are about thirty terrorists at the Market Square, according to the NSA. If we go down there with a couple hundred men, the enemy is going to sense danger. Somebody is bound to make a mistake. A little mistake, mind you, but a little one is all it'll take. Terrorists are paranoid bleeders. Anything that seems suspicious will trigger those sods either into bolting, or violence, or both."

"So what do you suggest?" Karista inquired, leaning against the edge of the desk. "You gentlemen are obviously more experienced in these matters than I am."

"A minimum number of good men—or women—is often the best choice for surveillance work," Katz explained. "That young fellow Kalevi seems to be a good man. A dozen operatives of his caliber would be good, or more than that provided you can get us some personnel who are skilled in the use of advanced surveillance equipment. Rifle microphones, light-density telescopes, lasers, that sort of thing."

"I think we can manage that," Karista said with a look of approval. "But I can't promise to get you anyone experienced in a firefight. Finland hasn't been involved in a war for almost fifty years. I'm afraid any veterans of the Russo-Finnish War would be a bit too old for this sort of mission. Some of them wouldn't be terribly happy to be working with Americans or Britons, either."

"Why not?" James asked, surprised by the remark. "Finland was protecting itself from invasion by Stalin's forces. The Americans and the British wouldn't have objected to a country opposing Communist invaders."

"The Americans and the British didn't take any official position during the first Russo-Finnish War in 1939," Karista explained. "But in 1941 both the United States and Great Britain were at war against the Axis powers, and Stalin was an ally in those days. The Soviets were fighting the Nazis. Finland, however, remained neutral during World War II, although we were involved with our own war with Russia. The Germans offered to support us against the Soviets, but my country refused. We did, however, let the Germans move troops through our country to attack Russia. Nonetheless, Great Britain declared war on Finland, and the United States severed relations with my country, and we had to surrender territory to Russia at the end of World War 11, which has always seemed unfair to us."

"A misunderstanding," Katz mused. "I can't say that I'd blame any veterans of the Russo-Finnish War for being a bit apprehensive about trusting Americans or Britons after such an experience. The fact that some people still mistakenly believe the Finns sided with the Nazis during the war probably doesn't make matters any better."

"So we won't have any blokes from the Russo-Finnish War working with us," McCarter growled, annoyed by the conversation. This was no time for a bloody history lesson, in the Briton's opinion. "Let's get together whatever qualified personnel are available and get those bastards."

"Don't get too anxious," Katz urged. "First, we have to make certain Valkeinen or any of his Red Ring comrades are even at the Market Square. Sanders's information could be wrong. I know you favor a direct approach, but we still have to make sure we have the right target before we move."

"And it would be better if we confronted the sons of bitches on our terms," James added. "Not theirs. Less chance of innocent bystanders getting hurt, and better chance of us catching Valkeinen and his cronies off guard. Remember, we want to get at least a couple of them alive."

"If they're as bonkers as that lot at the airport, that might not be so easy," McCarter replied, pacing the floor and furiously puffing on his cigarette. "Maybe we should check with that damn airfield and see if they've learned anything about the plane."

"They'll contact us," Karista assured him. "And aircraft will search Lappi to rescue your friends as soon as the weather breaks. I promise everything that can be done will be done."

"Of course," Katz said with a nod. "We'll just have to carry out our mission without them for now. Whatever circumstances they're faced with, they'll have to handle things on their own."

"If they're still alive," Karista said softly.

"Hey, they're still alive," James told him. "Until I see their bodies and declare them officially dead, our partners are *alive*, man."

"I understand how you feel," Karista said with a sigh. "But sometimes people just vanish in Lappi, and they're never seen again."

## 12

The wolf didn't taste so bad, after all, Rafael Encizo decided as he chewed a morsel skewered on the end of a pointed stick. The flavor was similar to roast goat. *Carne de cabra*, he thought. Rather tough and stringy *carne de cabra*. Some spices, a few corn tortillas and a couple of bottles of *cerveza* would have improved the meal. A bottle of tequila might even have made it desirable.

"That fire feels good," Rolf Lautanen said with a sigh of pleasure as he sat close to the blazing collection of spruce wood. "I didn't think you'd be able to get anything to burn in this weather."

"Probably couldn't if I used matches," Manning commented, carefully roasting more wolf meat over the campfire. "Luckily, that magnesium flare didn't go out because it is windy or damp. Pyrotechnics can be wonderful. I just wish I'd brought along more than two of them. Pencil detonators might work if we need a fire later."

"What other explosives do you have, Gary?" Encizo inquired, swallowing and trying not to think too much about what he was eating.

"Not much, I'm afraid," the Canadian demolitions expert answered. "I've got some C-4 plastic explosives inside my belt. Not a lot. I could knock down a couple trees with it if you want to start building that log cabin.''

"Do you always carry explosives?'' Lautanen asked in astonishment.

"Yeah,'' Manning replied with a shrug, as if carrying high explosives was as normal as wearing a wristwatch.

"Gary's never happy unless he's carrying something he might blow himself up with,'' Encizo commented.

"Gary and Rafael your real first names?'' Lautanen inquired as he pulled the wolfskin around his body. "I realize you're using false identification for the mission. I'm just curious.''

"Those are our real names,'' Encizo confirmed. "But we'd appreciate it if you don't share that with the SIA. Guess we let security slip a little.''

"Don't worry.'' The Finn smiled. "Your secret is safe with me. This wolf probably would have eaten me instead of the other way around if it wasn't for you two.''

"Hell,'' Manning muttered. "You wouldn't even be here if it weren't for us. Actually, if it wasn't for *me*. Coming to Lappi to search for bodies was my bright idea. I'm really sorry things worked out this way.''

"Nobody could have foreseen what would happen,'' Encizo told him. "I wonder who the hell sabotaged the plane.''

"Somebody at the airstrip,'' the Canadian replied, slowly turning the wooden spit just above the flames. "I'm sure that explosion in the wing engine wasn't an accident. Sounded like an oversize firecracker went off just before the fire occurred and the engine burst apart.''

Wolves howled in the distance. The three men glanced around nervously, expecting to see the sinister gray shapes of the predators. But nothing moved except the steady fall of sheets of snowflakes.

''I don't think they'll get close as long as the fire is burning,'' Manning remarked. ''But I'm not sure about trying to second-guess what these wolves might do anymore.''

''Well, I don't think any of us got much sleep,'' Encizo commented. ''I think we ought to take turns standing guard. That way, one or two of us can take advantage of the wolfskins and the fire to get some decent rest.''

''Not a bad idea,'' Manning agreed, pulling a piece of roast wolf from the end of the spit. ''We've all got some warm food in our bellies, too. That'll make us more comfortable while we relax.''

''Are you really going to eat more of that?'' Encizo asked, watching Manning consume another piece of meat.

''I guess I just wolfed it down,'' the Canadian said with a wry grin.

Encizo groaned at the pun, yet it was good to hear a joke under the circumstances. Even a bad pun was evidence that Manning hadn't lost his sense of humor—not that the stoic Canadian had ever had a future as a stand-up comic. If they could keep up their spirits while stuck in the middle of a frozen wasteland patrolled by a pack of killer wolves, Encizo figured, they were holding up pretty well.

"We still have lots of wolf meat left," the Canadian added. "It's not going to spoil very soon in this weather. That carcass still has enough meat for us to have a protein supply for a week, if we have to."

"A week of eating nothing but wolf meat?" Lautanen shook his head in dismay. "I hope someone rescues us before that happens. Preferably someone who brings us some cheese, some wine and some vegetables."

"Meantime we'll do what we must to survive," Encizo remarked, flexing his fingers near the campfire. The blaze was slowly dying, but the embers were still hot. "As long as a man still has the will to survive, he'll do whatever is needed to stay alive. When the will is gone, he'll just roll over and die. I've seen it before."

"This would be an easy place to die," Lautanen commented, staring out at the veil of falling snow. "I've heard that freezing to death isn't really such a bad way to die. Pretty uncomfortable for a while, but then your body goes numb, and you just go to sleep and never wake up."

"Oh, yeah?" Manning snorted. "Did you hear this story from somebody who actually froze to death?"

"Doesn't sound like a good way to die, in my opinion," Encizo remarked, glancing up at the black sky above. "I want to feel the sun on my face again. I want my flesh to be warm once more before it has to be cold for eternity. This might sound silly, but I don't want to die in the dark. Too much like being in the grave before you have to go into the ground."

"Well," Manning began, rubbing his left shoulder to help encourage the circulation of blood in his broken limb. ''None of us is dead yet, and as long as we keep our wits, I think we can get out of here alive.''

A wolf howled. The sound was closer than before and seemed more like a fierce challenge than a lonesome wail. The beast might have been contradicting Manning's remark, as if reminding the men that there were forces of nature that still intended to take their lives. Forces that killed with wind and cold. Forces that killed with claws and teeth.

ROLF LAUTANEN HAD RECEIVED the worst injury, and because of that he was allowed the longest rest period. Encizo and Manning constructed another crude hut of spruce branches around the injured Finn. Lautanen lay inside the shelter with the wolf pelt around his shivering body while the two Phoenix Force commandos stood guard.

The wolf pack remained near the camp, circling the area like four-legged buzzards waiting for a dying prey to finally expire. Encizo and Manning couldn't see the beasts due to the constant snowfall, which limited visibility. The wolves seemed to sense the potential danger of venturing any closer. Still, the Phoenix pair heard the soft growls and subdued barks of the pack. At least they thought they heard them. Perhaps it was just the wind howling, a sound as menacing as the wild carnivores that stalked them. The killer cold was as deadly as the wolves. Without decent shelter from the icy wind and the constant dampness of the snow-covered ground and the crystalline flakes in the sky, the risk of frostbite and hypothermia remained a serious threat.

Yet, Encizo and Manning knew they didn't imagine the nearness of the wolves. They sensed the presence of their bestial adversaries. The sixth sense of a combat veteran warned them of danger. They could almost hear the heartbeats of the wolves, feel the hunger of the predators and smell the excitement, the thrill of the hunt, the desire to bring down an opponent by force. The men of Phoenix Force understood these primitive emotions, for they, too, were hunters.

"This fire is just about gone," Manning muttered, glancing at the glowing remains of the camp fire.

"I'm surprised it lasted this long," Encizo added. A blanket of freshly fallen snow covered the pile of burnt wood. Melting snow had reduced most of the embers to wet ashes. Soon the last remnants of the fire would be snuffed out.

"How long has Rolf been asleep?" the Canadian inquired. Manning's wristwatch had been broken when the plane crashed.

"Almost four hours," Encizo answered, checking his Seiko diver's watch. "Let's wake him up, and you get some sleep next."

"You need it as much as I do," Manning replied.

"I don't have a busted flipper," the Cuban reminded him. "You got more reason to worry about getting frostbite in that broken arm, Gary. Rolf and I will take the next watch. You just get some rest and try to keep that arm as warm as possible."

"I'm not gonna argue," Manning said with a slight shrug. "But you guys be careful. The fire might have convinced those wolves to keep their distance. Better stay alert for them."

"Don't worry," Encizo assured him. "I don't think I'm gonna forget they're out there."

The two men woke Rolf Lautanen. The Finn reluctantly surrendered the wolf pelt to Manning and helped Encizo reconstruct the flimsy tree-branch shelter around the Canadian. Manning handed his Walther P-5 to Lautanen before he settled into the nest inside the crude hut.

"Snow hasn't stopped falling," Lautanen commented, gazing up at the sheets of white flakes. "Damn it. Can't even see the sky."

"If a plane passes over, we'll hear the engines," Encizo assured him. "Gary gave me a magnesium flare we can use to signal any aircraft that might show up. Meantime, keep an eye peeled for the big bad wolves."

"Still out there?" the Finn asked, leaning against his improvised crutch with one arm as he patted the reassuring bulge of the Walther pistol under his parka.

"Oh, yeah," Encizo confirmed. "We might be the only meal within a hundred kilometers. The wolves still seem to think they'll get us eventually."

"Maybe they're right," Lautanen remarked grimly.

"I don't need to hear that, Rolf," the Cuban told him. "This is nerve-racking enough without any conjecture of gloom and doom."

"Sorry," the Finnish agent replied. "I had a nightmare about those wolves. Guess I'm still a little rattled by it."

"I'm a little rattled just knowing those beasts are out there," Encizo admitted.

Suddenly they noticed a form approaching from the shadows. A long dark figure moved silently toward the camp, its pointed ears looking like antennas atop its thick head. Luminous eyes peered at the men, and it was as if the orbs were filled with a supernatural glow.

Lautanen gave an alarmed cry, drawing the Walther P-5 from his belt as he pointed at the wolf with his other hand.

Encizo's Heckler & Koch appeared in his hands. The Cuban drew the pistol with his right hand, reinforced the grip with his left and adopted a Weaver's stance in a smooth, fluid motion, pointing the weapon at the advancing wolf. The Cuban warrior held his fire and waited for a clear target to appear out of the vague shapes lurking behind the first animal.

Lautanen didn't hold his fire. The Finn hastily pulled the trigger of the unfamiliar Walther. The lead wolf loped sideways a fraction of a second before the pistol snarled. Encizo was certain the great dark beast was the same wolf he had fired at and missed when the pack had first attacked. The creature appeared to lead a charmed life. Lautanen's shot also missed the big beast. A bullet spat a harmless geyser of snow from the ground inches from the fleeing wolf.

Rolf Lautanen kept shooting. He was a dreadful marksman and fired the Walther too quickly, without taking time to aim. The Finn triggered four rounds. Wolves scattered as the gunshots roared, while one beast yelped with pain and thrashed around in the snow.

Several of the wolves fled, but three charged straight at the men. The powerful beasts bounded through the snow, their jaws open to reveal sharp teeth designed by nature to serve as deadly weapons. Lautanen fired another shot without proper care and pumped a bullet harmlessly into the snow near a wolf's charging feet.

Encizo's heart raced as another beast ran toward him, drool spewing from its open jaws. The furry shape bounced into the sights of the Heckler & Koch autoloader. The Phoenix pro squeezed the trigger twice. The wolf's body suddenly twisted in midair and collapsed on its side. Two bullets had pierced the animal's neck and severed its spinal cord.

Another wolf leaped over the body of the dead beast to launch itself at Encizo. The Cuban dropped to one knee and raised his pistol as the carnivore lunged. Encizo fired a parabellum slug between the beast's forelegs. He tried to aim for the wolf's heart, but he was unfamiliar with the anatomy of the animal and could only hope his aim was right on.

The bullet tore a merciless hole in the wolf's scapula and buried itself deep in the chest cavity. The wolf whimpered as its body spun in midair. Encizo pumped another 9 mm round into the beast's exposed belly. The wolf fell to the snow and landed on its back, its legs kicking wildly.

Lautanen emptied the last round from the magazine of the Walther autoloader and shot the third attacker as the beast closed in. The wolf tumbled onto its side, rolled in the snow and crawled upright to stand on three legs. A front leg had been shattered by Lautanen's bullet. The Finn realized he was out of ammunition and tossed the Walther aside to grip his crutch with both fists. Balancing himself awkwardly on one foot, he held the tree limb like a club and waited for the wolf to charge.

Wounded and crippled, the animal appeared to be frightened and angry. Since the crushed leg offered it little chance to flee, the wolf's instinct seemed to urge it to attack the man. The animal snarled at Lautanen, its ears flattened against its skull, the hairs rigid along its back and its formidable teeth displayed in a menacing challenge.

Remarkably fast, considering its ruined foreleg, the wolf lunged toward Lautanen. The SIA agent swung his cane, but the animal was faster and slammed into Lautanen before the man could swing the club. Man and beast fell to the snow-covered ground. Lautanen jammed a gloved fist into the wolf's open jaws to protect his face and neck from the terrible teeth. The beast bit hard and punctured cloth and skin.

Lautanen screamed as the powerful jaws closed with steel-trap force. Bones crunched in the Finn's hand. He beat at the wolf's head with his left fist, but the beast held on to its prey and swung its mighty skull back and forth. As the teeth ripped muscle and flesh, Lautanen's blood filled the animal's greedy mouth.

"My God!" Gary Manning exclaimed as he burst from the makeshift hut to see Lautanen locked in mortal combat with the wolf.

"Stand back!" Encizo shouted to his partner, then rushed forward and quickly knelt beside the struggling combatants. He jammed the muzzle of his H&K pistol into the side of the wolf's head and squeezed the trigger. A 9 mm slug knifed through the carnivore's brain and blasted a gory exit just below the right ear. Blood and gray matter spat from the wound. The wolf's corpse slumped across Lautanen's chest as the Finn trembled fearfully under the lifeless burden.

"Where's my gun?" Manning demanded. The big Canadian approached Lautanen and grabbed the dead wolf by the neck. Even with just one good arm, the burly Manning had no trouble pulling the animal's corpse away from Lautanen's chest.

The SIA agent wasn't paying attention to Manning's words. Clutching his crushed right hand in his left palm, blood dripping between his fingers, the Finn rolled on his belly to jam the mutilated extremity into the snow.

"I think Rolf ran out of ammo and tossed the piece," Encizo supplied, glancing around to be certain the other wolves hadn't decided to launch another assault. "I was sort of busy myself at the time."

"Hell," Manning rasped through clenched teeth. "That was about the dumbest thing he could have done."

"He's suffered enough," Encizo said, kneeling next to Lautanen to examine the man's wounded hand. "This looks pretty bad."

"Doesn't look too good for any of us," the Canadian commented, scanning the area apprehensively.

"Yeah," Encizo began as he reached inside his parka to tear strips of cloth from his shirt. "But you and I didn't have three fingers bitten off."

"God," Manning whispered, gazing at the bloodied stumps of Lautanen's fingers. Only the index finger had been spared by the wolf's vengeful jaws. "Poor bastard might go into shock. I'll get the blanket."

Encizo used the strips of cloth from his shirt to bind an emergency bandage around the Finn's mangled hand. He glanced over his shoulder frequently, half expecting the wolves to strike again while they were busy tending to the wounded Finn. However, the beasts didn't attack, although Encizo felt certain the pack hadn't ventured far.

This place is killing us a little at a time, Encizo thought grimly. It seemed they were being whittled down bit by bit, until soon there would be no way to fight back. No way to survive.

## 13

Erik Valkeinen didn't look like a terrorist leader. Forty-one years old and still athletically trim, Valkeinen had curly blond hair and a small bow mouth, which gave him the look of a cupid. Many women described him as "cute." The females who had been involved with him—and there had been many—generally felt that Erik was a lot of fun most of the time, but he tended to indulge in too many practical jokes for any mature woman to consider him a choice for a long-term relationship. Not that he seemed to have any interest in a permanent involvement with any woman.

But Valkeinen's employers only had occasion to praise his professionalism while on the job. Valkeinen worked as a maintenance engineer at a major chemical corporation in Helsinki. He was never late for work, generally got along well with the other employees and always did his job with cool efficiency. He didn't gamble, use drugs, smoke cigarettes or drink to excess. On the surface, Erik Valkeinen appeared to be a model employee and a good citizen. A fun-loving bachelor who still had a schoolboy's sense of humor.

It was no wonder that the Security Intelligence Agency had never suspected him of being connected with the Red War Ring terrorist movement. Most terrorists have difficulty associating with other people or maintaining a job for any length of time. Their single-minded fanaticism and extremist political views tend to make them undesirable company and unreliable workers. Either the man was smart enough to put up a convincing cover or the National Security Agency was wrong about the guy, Katz and Calvin James had concluded after checking into Valkeinen's background.

"You think Sanders might be full of shit?" Calvin James asked as he sat in the back of a blue-and-green van with Katz and the SIA agent they knew as Kalevi.

"Probably," Katz replied with a shrug. "But he might be right about Valkeinen."

"The NSA was right about the Red Ring fanatics gathering in this area," Kalevi remarked as he peered through a surveillance telescope mounted in the roof of the van. "We've identified ten known members of the terrorist group already."

The van was one of seven surveillance vehicles at the Kauppatori Square near the South Harbor of Helsinki. Armed with special binoculars, hidden telescopes, rifle microphones and high-intensity amplifiers, Orm Karista's agents were scattered throughout the area. All were busy trying to locate and identify members of the Red War Ring alleged to be in the area.

That was no simple task. As Karista had predicted, the Kauppatori was indeed crowded. More than a thousand tourists and almost as many Finns shuffled from shop to shop. Street merchants offered a variety of goods and refreshments. The scene reminded Katz of the Grand Bazaar in Istanbul. The Kauppatori wasn't as large as the famous Turkish market square, of course, yet the colorful setting and good-natured haggling about prices were very similar. The Kauppatori reflected the nature of the Finnish people—hardworking, intelligent, basically friendly toward visitors yet shrewd in matters of business.

Courage was another national trait of the Finns, Katz reflected. Surveillance of terrorists can be very dangerous, and confronting them with the intention of taking prisoners is certainly no job for cowards. Karista had had no trouble getting volunteers for the mission. The SIA personnel were all experienced in "sneaking and peeking," but none were combat veterans. Katz wasn't worried that any of the men and women on the surveillance team would be spotted by the terrorists. The SIA people were good at conventional spy-versus-spy operations. With the Soviet Union for a neighbor, they had to be. However, if guns came out, the odds would be in the favor of the terrorists.

The Red Ring fanatics were probably no more skilled with weapons than the SIA personnel, but the terrorists would be less hesitant to use their weapons. The agents had to worry about innocent bystanders and bad publicity, while neither issue concerned the terrorists one iota. The terrorists already had murder in their hearts, and some of them had probably taken human lives before. The majority of the SIA agents didn't even carry guns on most assignments, and many hadn't fired a weapon for years. Not exactly the sort of unit Phoenix Force would have chosen for support in a firefight.

Yet the SIA surveillance people had done a good job of spotting Erik Valkeinen and several of his Red Ring comrades. A pair of supersnoops had trained a laser mike on a window of Valkeinen's apartment on Norra Esplanaden. A high-tech version of the rifle microphone, the device projected a laser beam that received vibrations from the room against the glass. These vibrations were then transmitted to a special radio receiver used by the surveillance team.

With the aid of the listening device, they had discovered that Valkeinen was discussing a mission with three or more individuals in his apartment. The group had failed to mention any details of the secret plot, but the SIA snoops reported that Valkeinen had asked his lieutenants if all their comrades were properly armed with adequate ammunition.

Apparently, Phoenix Force and the SIA had arrived at a very opportune time. The terrorists seemed to be planning a hit, and all evidence suggested they intended to go into action soon.

"Eagle Eye to Ground Control," David McCarter's voice crackled from a radio inside the surveillance van containing Katz, James and Kalevi. "You blokes read me? Over."

"Loud and clear, Eagle Eye," James spoke into the radio. "What's up, man? Over."

"Spotted curly-top and at least six of his mates," the Briton replied, referring to Valkeinen and some other Red Ring terrorists. "They're all headed toward the harbor. Every one of those bleeders is carrying some sort of luggage. Briefcase, duffel bag, backpack. Every one has something to carry more than some sandwiches in...."

"Are you certain they're all moving toward the harbor?" Katz interrupted, taking the radio mike from James.

"Affirmative," McCarter confirmed. "Better figure there's more of them I haven't spotted yet. Sure as hell looks like something coming down right now. Over."

"Understood, Eagle Eye," Katz stated. "Stay on them, but don't get too close. Don't want to ruin any surprises. Over."

"I just hope we'll be the only blokes to pull any surprises," McCarter answered. "Over and out."

The British ace had reported his news from a Lynx helicopter that was slowly circling the Kauppatori area. The chopper towed a long banner advertising a popular brand of West German snow tires so the aircraft wouldn't appear suspicious as it hovered in the twilight sky above the Market Square and allowed McCarter his "Eagle Eye" view of the district.

"Kalevi," Katz said sharply, "tell the driver to head for the harbor immediately. Whatever the Red War Ring plans to do today, they're getting ready to carry it out now."

"Right," the Finnish agent replied with a nod.

"At least the harbor isn't in the heart of a busy market center," Calvin James began as he opened a metal locker to take his M-16 assault rifle from the case. "Not as many innocent bystanders to worry about."

"That's what bothers me," Katz said grimly, gazing at a map of Helsinki on a corkboard on the wall. "The terrorists have been attacking targets in well-populated areas in order to score large body counts with each hit. Why are they apparently moving from the Market Square?''

"To discuss strategy?" James suggested as he pulled back the charging handle of his M-16 to chamber the first round.

"I doubt that," the Israeli said thoughtfully, still examining the map. "Valkeinen seems to have just completed a meeting with his lieutenants, and they appeared to have a plan already worked out. Besides, they've got a lot of Red Ring fanatics carrying luggage which probably contains weapons. They wouldn't have that much firepower just to discuss strategy...."

Katz raised his right arm and placed the steel hooks of his prosthesis on the map. He slid the hooks to the edge of South Harbor. A small circle containing the letter *L* marked a spot on the shoreline.

"Kalevi—" Katz turned to the Finnish agent, who had just returned from speaking with the driver "—what does this stand for?"

"*Lautta,*" Kalevi answered. "The ferry. You see, ferryboats transport people across the harbor to the islands. Valkosarri, Ryssansarri, Luoto, or one can even travel by ferry all the way to Sweden."

"Are any of these islands well populated, or is any historic site located on any of the islands?" Katz asked. "Something that would upset the Finnish people if it was destroyed or seized by terrorists? Especially a site that is frequently visited by both Finns and tourists."

"Suomenlinna," Kalevi declared without hesitation. "It is an ancient island fortress that has been converted into a recreation center."

"That sounds familiar," Katz remarked. "Is Suomenlinna also known as the Gibraltar of the North?"

"We Finns don't call it that, but I suppose they might use that expression in parts of southern Europe," Kalevi replied. "Suomenlinna was built in 1748, and the island fortress was never taken by siege. Now it has parks and restaurants and cultural centers. You think the terrorists are headed there?"

"I'd be surprised if Suomenlinna wasn't their target," Katz replied as he reached for the radio transmitter. The Phoenix commander switched it on. "Eagle Eye, this is Ground Control. Come on. Over."

"Eagle Eye," David McCarter's voice replied. "Read you loud and clear. Over."

"Head directly for Suomenlinna Island," Katz instructed. "Your copilot ought to know where it is. The place is a recreation center, so it must have a security guard force. Tell them to get ready for trouble—serious trouble. Over."

"So that's curly-top's destination?" McCarter mused. "We'll arrange a nice reception for them, Ground Control."

"There is a possibility I've guessed wrong," Katz warned. "We should know for certain by the time you reach the island. Probably there will be a lot of civilians in the area. You know what that means. Over."

"I understand, Ground Control," the Briton assured him.

"Bear in mind this is a sensitive situation," Katz urged, painfully aware that tact wasn't one of McCarter's strengths. The British ace was intelligent enough to handle the situation with more diplomacy than usual, however.

"I'll take care of my part," McCarter assured him.

"We'll try to do ours, too, Eagle Eye," Katz stated. "Take care. Over and out."

ERIK VALKEINEN and his Red War Ring comrades boarded the ferry bound for Suomenlinna, just as Katz had predicted. The surveillance van arrived at the harbor just as the terrorists were buying tickets for their trip. Kalevi observed the group mounting the ramp to the ferry.

"We have agents posted by the motorboats farther down the pier," Kalevi announced, taking his Lahti pistol from shoulder leather to work the slide, chamber a round and switch on the safety. "We can contact the harbor patrol and reinforce them with our own people in powerboats to surround the ferry and force the terrorists to surrender."

"No good, man," Calvin James remarked as he slid his M-16 into a canvas carrying case. "There are too many civilians aboard that ferry. The terrorists would have a boatload of hostages. We'd have to hold our fire until we could get a decent shot, but they'd be free to blow us out of the water with whatever sort of hardware they might have. And we don't know what that might be. Those bastards could have rocket launchers for all we know."

"I've contacted Eagle Eye at Suomenlinna," Katz announced, taking an Uzi submachine gun from the weapons rack. "He'll set up a defense at the island. Our odds will be better if we hit the enemy there."

Katz, James and Kalevi left the van and headed for the rental motorboats farther down the harbor piers. Two SIA agents were stationed there. They had been placed at the boats in case the terrorists bolted from the Market Square and tried to seize the boats to escape. The precaution offered Phoenix Force an unexpected advantage when the Red Ring members threw them a curve.

The two Phoenix Force members and Kalevi climbed into a powerboat and started the motor. Fortunately, no one had wanted to rent a boat to cruise the harbor due to the harsh cold and biting wind. The waters were a bit choppy and hardly the type of atmosphere to lure tourists or amateur fishermen to venture into the Gulf of Finland.

"We're not going to try to take them on our own," Kalevi began, pushing down on his fur hat to keep the wind from ripping the headgear from his skull. He sounded as if he thought they were headed for a suicide mission.

"Reinforcements will follow," Katz assured him, tucking his Uzi under a canvas tarp as the powerboat sped out across the harbor bay. "But we couldn't send a dozen boats filled with agents and harbor patrol officers. The terrorists would be suspicious if an armada suddenly appeared alongside the ferry."

Calvin James piloted the powerboat with ease despite the rough waves. The former SEAL had handled similar vessels in worse conditions. The smaller powerboat soon cut through the frigid waters to cruise past the slower ferryboat. Some of the passengers lined the handrail to watch the powerboat jet by. James barely glanced up at the ferry. He didn't want Valkeinen and his comrades to wonder why a black man was piloting the smaller, swifter vessel.

"Wave at the nice people," James urged as he steered the powerboat around the ferry.

Katz and Kalevi raised their arms and waved at the ferry. A dozen arms waved back. Katz smiled as he waved his left arm from side to side. He wondered how many of the smiling faces of the passengers who were returning the greeting belonged to Red Ring terrorists.

The powerboat continued to speed through the water and passed the ferry. It rapidly gained on the big passenger vessel, then vanished from the view of the ferry. Icy water splashed over the stem. The three men shivered as the cold wind seemed to penetrate their clothes and skin.

"I just thought of something awful," James remarked, shaking his head to toss off clammy moisture from his face and the hood of his parka. "What if the bastards hijack the ferry and force it to go to another island instead of Suomenlinna?"

"I wish you hadn't said that," Katz admitted with a frown as the boat moved on to approach the island fortress of Suomenlinna. From a distance, the site resembled Alcatraz: a mountain of stone structures jutted from the sea. Yet Suomenlinna was more than a century older than the infamous island prison in San Francisco Bay. The walls of Suomenlinna revealed a definite European style, with their stone and mortar and a great towering stone keep.

The boat pulled in to the pier to the island. Katz and Kalevi climbed from the vessel, and James tossed them a line to moor the boat. Then he handed them the weapon cases and climbed onto the pier. All of them headed up the path toward the fortress.

"About bloody time you got here," David Mc-Carter announced as he appeared from the entrance.

The Briton was also dressed in an olive-drab parka with a fur-lined hood. He wore a web belt around his waist with the Browning 9 mm pistol in a cross-draw holster, accompanied by magazine pouches and grenades. An Ingram M-10 machine pistol hung from a shoulder strap near his right hip.

"Traffic was a bitch," James replied, gazing across the walls of the fortress. "How well is everything set up for the guests of honor?"

"Could be better," the Briton said with a shrug. "The security force here isn't equipped to deal with this sort of thing. Not very well armed. The guards have some handguns and shotguns and a couple of bolt-action rifles that are basically kept in the armory in case there's some sort of rabid animal."

"What about the civilians?" Katz asked as they followed McCarter back to the mouth of the fortress.

"They've been herded into a reinforced section of the fortress," McCarter answered. "Probably the safest spot on the island, unless explosions send the walls crashing down on them."

"Cheerful notion," Katz said dryly. "Well, we'd better get ready, because the ferry will arrive in a few minutes and we don't know what the enemy will throw at us. Whatever it is, we'd better be ready for it."

## 14

Rafael Encizo groaned as he firmly held the corpse of another wolf while Gary Manning cut into it. With three more dead wolves to skin and butcher, Encizo feared his partner would be cooking wolf steaks for the next six months. The Cuban warrior didn't feel hungry enough to welcome a diet of wolf meat. He was beginning to wonder if the bark from spruce trees might be edible.

"Okay," Manning began, cradling his broken arm with his right, the blood-stained Tanto still clutched in his fist. "We've got another wolfskin blanket."

He pried back the animal hide with the blade. Encizo gathered up the fresh wolfskin and carried it to Rolf Lautanen. He lay on a carpet of spruce branches with the first pelt draped over him. Encizo placed the second skin over the agent, the furry side next to his trembling body.

"No," Lautanen croaked softly. "You two need to stay warm, too...."

"You're injured worse than either of us," Manning stated as he stepped over the pink-and-gray form of the freshly skinned animal. "You've also lost a lot of blood. You need to rest and stay as warm as possible."

"I haven't been much help to you," Lautanen said sadly. "I'm sorry. Sorry to be a burden and sorry I did so poorly when the wolves attacked. Lost the gun..."

"Don't worry about that," Encizo urged. "None of us are perfect, thank God. I've made some mistakes here, too."

"What mistake did you make?" Lautanen asked.

"To begin with, I volunteered," the Cuban replied with a feeble grin.

"Hey," Manning began as he waded through thigh-deep snow to join the others. "You notice something? It's stopped snowing."

The Canadian was right, Encizo realized. The sky was still dark, but the sheets of falling snow had finally ceased. They saw the stars shining brightly above like a thousand beacons in the night sky. A sliver of a crescent moon cast a pale light across the white surface of the ground below.

*"Cristo,"* Encizo muttered, gazing up at the welcome view of heavenly bodies above. "When did the snow stop?"

"I don't know," Manning admitted. "I just noticed it myself. We've all been so busy, I guess we didn't realize it until now."

"If the snowstorms don't start again, the weather will be more advantageous for a rescue plane to be sent to look for us," Lautanen declared.

"Yeah," Manning agreed, shuffling through the snow toward the site of the plane wreckage. "Let's make sure they don't miss us."

"What have you got in mind?" Encizo inquired, plodding through the white drifts behind the Canadian.

"Let's haul out some of this junk and make use of it," Manning suggested. "We've got nice long sections of the wings and the carriage. Wide and long pieces will work best. Try to find dark sections of metal and plastic. Those will show up best in the snow."

"A sign," Encizo said, understanding what Manning had in mind. "We'll use the portions of the plane to write out an SOS."

"Exactly," Manning confirmed. He turned back toward Lautanen. "How do you say 'help' in Finnish, Rolf?"

*"Auttaa,"* the SIA agent replied as he sat up to watch them.

"Hope we can find enough junk to write that," Encizo muttered as they searched through the wreckage for suitable pieces. "How do you spell that, Rolf?"

*"Auttaa!"* Lautanen shouted.

"Yeah," Encizo began as he turned to glare at the Finnish agent. "How do you spell—"

Suddenly Encizo saw that Lautanen wasn't just repeating the word for help. The sinister shapes of the hungry pack had returned. The wolves approached slowly, moving easily through the dense snow as moonlight gently bathed their sleek gray figures with a soft glow. The wolves seemed ghostlike, supernatural creatures that had inspired tales of werewolves and countless nightmares.

The pack moved toward Lautanen, sensing the vulnerability of the wounded Finn. They smelled blood, and their jaws hung open in expectation. The fresh meat of the dead wolves also seemed to excite them, and some of the carnivores sank sharp teeth into the carcass. Two of the beasts pulled the remains away from the rest of the pack, but three more wolves soon rushed forward to try to claim part of the prize. One beast limped after them, dragging a damaged hind leg. It was the wolf Lautanen had wounded with a poorly placed 9 mm in the flank.

The rest of the pack showed little interest in their slain brethren. Wolves are highly social animals that get along well with their own species within a particular pack, and cannibalism is rare among them. Perhaps wolves, like man, tend to find the practice of feeding on their own species repulsive. Some of the wolves appeared to be more willing to break this taboo than others. The majority of the pack still seemed to regard the three men as their rightful prey.

Encizo drew his Heckler & Koch pistol. Since they had been unable to find Manning's Walther P-5, the Cuban's gun was the only firearm they had left. Manning had given him the 9 mm parabellum cartridges from the spare magazine of his Walther. Encizo had a total of eighteen rounds left. He counted nine wolves. Half of these seemed willing to settle for cannibalizing the wolf carcass. That left only four or five to deal with.

The Cuban frowned. He didn't see the big dark gray brute among the pack, the bold and swift creature that seemed more aggressive than the others. So far it had been too fast for the bullets fired in its direction. Encizo felt that the dark beast was the leader of the pack, although he had no solid reason for believing that.

Maybe if he killed the leader the rest of the pack would flee and hesitate to continue the hunt. What do

wolf packs do when they lose a leader, Encizo wondered. Is there a second-in-command to take over, or
do the wolves have to determine who is the new boss?
Encizo had no idea what the wolves might do.

"What are you waiting for?" Lautanen demanded. "Shoot, damn it. Shoot!"

"Don't worry," Encizo replied, holding the H&K in
a firm two-handed grip. "I'll nail the first furry bastard that gets any closer."

Manning pried loose a foot of steel rod from the
plane wreckage. That was no easy task for a man with
a broken arm, but the Canadian was a powerful man,
and his single arm was stronger than the two limbs of
most men.

"Improvise," Manning grunted as he yanked the
makeshift weapon from the wreckage.

"Where's the dark wolf?" Encizo wondered aloud,
gazing at the sinister yellow eyes of the pack.

A loud growl erupted from behind Encizo, and he
turned sharply as a large dark gray shape bolted toward him. The big wolf lunged as Encizo swung his
pistol to track the hurtling form. He snap-aimed the
H&K autoloader and squeezed the trigger.

The wolf howled, and its body jackknifed in midair as a parabellum slug tore into its upper left foreleg. The animal's momentum didn't let up, however,
and the wolf slammed into Encizo before he could
dodge. The impact knocked Encizo's feet from under
him, and man and beast fell into the snow in a kicking, snarling heap.

Two more wolves followed the big dark beast. One
joined in the attack on Encizo while the other charged
toward Gary Manning. The Canadian warrior read-

ied himself for the attacking beast with the steel rod in
his right fist. He stood his ground and allowed the
wolf to close in before he swung the improvised club
with all his might.

The rod struck the snarling wolf between its pointed
ears. The animal fell sideways in the snow, feet paw-
ing wildly and jaws snapping at Manning's legs. The
ferocious teeth tore at the thick leather of the Phoenix pro's boot. Manning immediately struck the wolf
again. The beast yelped as steel smashed into its hard
skull.

Dazed, the wolf skidded on its belly. Manning
caught up with the beast with two long strides and
quickly swung his arm with the rod clenched in the
center in his fist. He drove one end of the steel pole
into the base of the wolf's skull, just above a thick tuft
of fur. Bone cracked, and the animal's spinal cord
snapped like a taut thread. The wolf twitched slightly
and sprawled dead in the snow.

"Jesus," Manning rasped as he glanced up to see
that the first group of wolves had decided to join the
attack.

Lautanen let out a cry of terror as three wolves descended upon him. The Finnish agent tried to flee, but
he was too weak to rise even with the assistance of his
crutch. He crawled as best he could, but his wounded
leg and maimed hand slowed him as much as the
snowy bog.

A wolf lunged, its jaws open to display daggerlike
teeth. Lautanen lashed out with his crutch and struck
the beast across the muzzle. It whimpered like a startled dog and recoiled. Another wolf pounced, its paws
landing on Lautanen's chest and driving the breath

from his lungs. The beast snapped its powerful jaws around the SIA agent's neck and sunk sharp teeth into soft flesh.

Manning hesitated, unsure of which man to help first. Lautanen was in serious trouble. So was Enzizo. The Cuban struggled with the big charcoal-colored beast as another wolf pranced about near Enzizo's head, snarling as it tried to locate a clear target. Despite his desperate situation, Enzizo still had a better chance than Lautanen. Enzizo still held a pistol in his fist, although his arm was pinned down by the weight of the dark wolf, and he still had full use of both arms and legs. The same wasn't true of poor Rolf Lautanen.

Reluctantly Manning abandoned his partner and stomped through the snow to assist the Finnish agent. Two wolves were tearing at Lautanen's still body. A third animal held the Finn's right ankle in its jaws and chewed a bloody chunk from the limb.

Lautanen didn't cry out. Manning's stomach knotted with revulsion when he realized why. Rolf Lautanen's throat had been ripped out. It was too late to rescue the SIA agent. Manning wondered what Lautanen had thought before he died. The agent's death must have been relatively swift, yet Rolf had certainly realized he was dying. His terror must have been mind shattering. Or had the pain from the tearing jaws blotted out all other sensations? What was it like to literally have one's life ripped out by wild beasts?

Manning had seen men die many times before, but he had seldom seen one killed in such a brutal manner. Worse, Manning realized that he might soon share Lautanen's fate. Two predators approached the Canadian slowly, shuffling forward on silent paws. The wolves' backs were arched, their bodies coiled and ready to spring. Strings of saliva dripped from their open jaws as they ventured closer.

RAFAEL ENCIZO WAS UNAWARE of the plight of his companions. The entire universe consisted of his own personal survival at that moment. All that existed was Encizo's struggle to stay alive as he wrestled with one wolf while another tried to clamp its murderous teeth around his neck or some other vulnerable target.

The dark wolf thrashed wildly in Encizo's grasp. The Cuban had managed to wrap his left arm around the beast's neck and keep the canine from using its jaws. The Cuban realized he couldn't hold on to the wolf much longer. It was too strong, too large, and the wound in the beast's foreleg only served to make it more desperate and more determined to break free.

Suddenly Encizo's right arm slipped free of the weight of the struggling dark wolf. He raised his fist, the Heckler & Koch held ready. Encizo prepared to jam the pistol into the skull of the dark beast to dispatch the animal with a 9 mm slug, but the second wolf lunged, attempting to bite the Cuban's wrist.

Encizo adroitly shifted the aim of his pistol and thrust the barrel between the beast's sharp teeth. The wolf's jaws clamped metal, and Encizo squeezed the trigger. A bullet burst through the roof of the predator's upper jaw. The parabellum round entered the creature's skull and burned through its brain. An exit hole as big as a quarter appeared at the top of the wolf's head as a flow of crimson and gray spewed from the wound.

Encizo's pistol was still lodged in the dead animal's jaws, frozen in a firm death grip. The dark beast was struggling even more forcefully than before, startled by the report of Encizo's pistol. The Cuban's grip on the wolf's neck began to slip. He pulled the pistol, but it refused to slide free from the dead carnivore's teeth.

*"Madre de Dios,"* Encizo hissed through clenched teeth as he released the H&K and suddenly wrapped his legs around the dark wolf's torso.

Man and beast rolled violently in the snow. Encizo pressed his forearm against the wolf's lower jaw to try to control the animal's head. His right hand groped for the Gerber Mark I dagger in his boot sheath.

His fingers touched the familiar cast-aluminum handle of the knife. Encizo unsnapped the retaining strap with a flick of his thumb and pulled the dagger from leather. He felt the wolf's head shift from his grasp, but kept his legs coiled around the animal and turned to shove it face first into the snow.

The wolf uttered a muffled snarl. Encizo quickly raised the Gerber and thrust the point of the blade into a pointed ear. Sharp steel sunk into the cavity, penetrating the ear and piercing the animal's brain. The shaggy beast convulsed in Encizo's grip, bucking and trembling between his legs. The animal's death throes seemed an obscene parody of the sex act, and Encizo broke free of the death embrace, disgusted by the contact with the dying beast.

Encizo gasped for breath and tried to control his shaky hands as he crawled to the pistol, which was still gripped in the jaws of the other dead wolf. He glanced up to see Manning about to be attacked by two more beasts. The rest of the pack seemed to be busy feasting on the corpse of Lautanen, except for two wolves that appeared satisfied with the skinned carcass.

Gary Manning blocked an attacking wolf with a blow from his steel rod. The animal's reflexes were remarkable. It managed to clamp its teeth on the improvised weapon and hold on to the rod as another wolf leaped forward. Another set of deadly teeth rocketed toward the Canadian's face.

Manning dropped to one knee and ducked his head. The airborne wolf sailed over his crouched form and landed in the snow behind him. The Phoenix fighter released the rod, which was still held fast by the jaws of the other wolf. He rolled away from the beasts. White-hot pain shot from his broken forearm when the limb struck the ground. Manning tried to ignore the pain and reached inside his parka.

The Phoenix veteran grasped the hilt of the Cold Steel Tanto and withdrew the thick steel blade as one beast attacked and the other prepared to follow its partner's example. Manning surprised the attacking wolf by lunging forward, as well. The Canadian and his canine opponent crashed together like a pair of locomotives going in opposite directions on the same track.

Man and animal collided and fell to the snow. Manning landed on top of the wolf and shoved the beast backward into the white drifts as he drove the Tanto blade deep between the wolf's front legs. Hot blood poured across Manning's fist and wrist as the steel weapon punctured the animal's heart.

The second wolf sprang from the ground and launched itself at the Canadian's broad back. A pistol shot barked in the night air, and a hollowpoint round smashed into the side of the leaping beast's skull. Bone cracked, and the animal fell lifeless to the ground.

Manning glanced over his shoulder. Encizo had pried his H&K autoloader from the jaws of the beast that had seemed so stubborn even in death. The Cuban climbed to his feet slowly and staggered toward the remaining wolves in the pack.

The pistol shots had frightened the animals, and the pack had chosen retreat as the logical choice of action. Only one beast remained by the body of Rolf Lautanen, chewing on the dead man's flesh. Encizo shuffled closer, both hands locked around the grips of his pistol. The wolf lowered its ears and bared its teeth in a menacing growl.

"Think you're tough?" Encizo sneered as if speaking to a human opponent. "Try this."

He aimed carefully and placed a slug between the wolf's yellow eyes. The animal fell across the corpse of Rolf Lautanen. The rest of the pack howled and whimpered, dashing from the scene of the carnage. The animal with the wounded flank stumbled along behind the others. Encizo considered shooting the beast, but held his fire.

"God," Manning muttered as he scooped up a handful of snow and wiped it across his sweat-bathed forehead. "That was too close, amigo."

"Yeah," the Cuban agreed, lowering his pistol. "Let's put together that sign and hope somebody finds us soon. I'm not sure we can survive another attack if those wolves come back again."

## 15

The ferry arrived at Suomenlinna. Erik Valkeinen's bow mouth puckered into a pout. The expression didn't betray his anxiety as he stared at the pier along the shore of the island fortress. The Red War Ring leader sensed that something was wrong. He was a careful man. He had to be to have remained in control of the terrorist outfit for so many years. Valkeinen had also developed strong survival instincts, and these protective senses were ringing alarm bells inside his head as he peered out at Suomenlinna.

The pier was quiet and empty, except for two men on the wide boardwalk. They wore badges on their fur-lined caps. Security officers, Valkeinen realized. He had made the trip to and from Suomenlinna twice before in preparation for the mission, and he recognized the uniforms of the security patrol stationed on the island. Most didn't carry weapons, and none were authorized to carry anything more lethal than a handgun.

The deserted pier worried Valkeinen. Where were the tourists and sightseers? The ferry brought people to the island and took others back to the mainland. Yet, the previous group of visitors weren't waiting on the pier to return to the South Harbor. Something was definitely wrong.

But Valkeinen saw no evidence of any police or military ambush. The terrorist leader raised a pair of binoculars to his eyes and scanned the area. He found no uniformed figures lurking among the rocks or police snipers stationed along the walls of the fortress. Surely two security guards wouldn't have been sent to deal with the Red Ring hit team. Their plot still appeared to be a secret, but the guards might intend to conduct some sort of security check.

Perhaps the security personnel had decided to inspect suspicious baggage for weapons or explosives as a precaution due to concern about terrorist activity. Damnation, Valkeinen thought grimly. Damn Bajanov and the other KGB officers who wanted results too quickly. Too much had been happening too fast. The airport incident was proof of that. Valkeinen had been opposed to carrying out the Suomenlinna operation until they had more time to plan the mission, but Major Kharkov had insisted the assault commence on schedule.

Valkeinen despised Kharkov. That smug bastard didn't care about anything. Kharkov wasn't a devout Communist or a warrior of the revolution. He was nothing but a murderer who happened to be working for Moscow instead of a gangster syndicate. The assassin always seemed amused by missions concerning death. Kharkov and his two stooges, Larrs and Olav, thought they were professionals giving orders to the amateur members of the Red War Ring. The amateurs were always expendable.

Kharkov's reasons had been sound, however. The airport failure had been a major defeat, a blow to the morale of the revolutionary forces. They needed a big success to restore the confidence of their followers and to maintain the terror felt by their enemies. The Finnish government and the general public couldn't be allowed to think that the revolution could fail or that the terror tactics of the urban guerrillas could be effectively countered by antiterrorist forces. A major victory was needed, and the quicker the better.

As the two security officers began to climb on board the ferryboat, Valkeinen and the other Red Ring terrorists stiffened. Some of them began to reach for weapons, but Valkeinen had assigned more responsible Ring lieutenants to supervise smaller teams. They prevented the hotheads from drawing weapons until Valkeinen ordered them to do so.

The terrorist leader feared he might have to do exactly that. If the two half-witted security guards intended to search the passengers for suspicious carry-on luggage, the Red Ring terrorists would be forced to use their weapons. Gunshots would surely alert the other security personnel within the fortress, and they would radio the mainland for assistance. Valkeinen and the other terrorists would soon be trapped on the island, surrounded by police and military vessels.

Most terrorists boast that they are willing, if not eager, to die for their cause. Valkeinen had once shared that notion, but he had become more cynical about the righteous nature of the "revolution" and less trusting of the KGB "advisers" who manipulated many terrorist outfits throughout Western Europe. He didn't want to die for Bajanov or Kharkov or whoever the bastard was who had dreamed up this phase of the operation. Valkeinen planned to retire and start a new life in the Republic of Ireland, far from troubled Belfast. First he had to get off the island of Suomenlinna alive.

Kalevi, dressed as a security patrolman, began by holding up his gloved hands to get the attention of the passengers as he addressed them. "Please, may I have your attention, ladies and gentlemen. There will be a slight delay before the tour of the Suomenlinna fortress begins."

"Is something wrong, Officer?" the head of a tour group inquired nervously. She was the guide for a group of tourists from America, Britain, France and Belgium. The woman didn't want to have to translate bad news into two languages. The recent terrorist activity had hurt the tourism in Finland, and the guide prayed nothing had happened to make it worse.

"An accident occurred," Kalevi explained, stepping to the bow of the boat. "No one was hurt, but there is a possibility that a portion of our regular tour will have to be postponed due to need for repairs."

"Where are the passengers for the trip back to the South Harbor?" the ferryboat captain asked in a subdued voice, trying to conceal his apprehension from the crowd.

"Part of a rampart collapsed," Kalevi answered. "It blocked the path for the tour group already inside the fortress. They're safe inside a corner tower, but we have to clear away rubble and make certain the path is safe before we bring them out of there."

"Does that mean the tour is canceled?" Valkeinen inquired as he approached the two uniformed figures.

The other "security guard" was David McCarter. The Briton didn't understand a word of Finnish, but he realized Valkeinen had asked a question. McCarter simply shrugged in reply and continued to watch the passengers. His right hand remained in a coat pocket and rested on the comforting grips of his Browning Hi-Power 9 mm pistol.

"Whether this group will be able to conduct a tour of the fortress will depend on whether or not the maintenance engineers find any evidence of risk from weather wear in other parts of the buildings," Kalevi answered. "Meantime, we'd like to take you all to the best restaurant on the island so you may wait in comfort. Beverages will be served free of cost, and we apologize for the inconvenience."

The passengers filed off the ferry and followed the security guards to the entrance of the fortress. Someone asked McCarter another question, and the Briton shrugged in response. He hoped the passenger hadn't asked what his name was or some other question that only a moron wouldn't be able to answer. The tour group probably figured McCarter was just rude. The Briton wasn't very concerned about that, so long as the terrorists among the party didn't get suspicious of the silent patrolman.

They headed through the archway in the fortress walls and moved across the wide parade field within the compound. The ancient stone walls and billets loomed above them. Floodlights and indoor lighting were supplied by electrical generators on the island. A flanking tower had been converted into a cultural museum, and a pleasant restaurant had been constructed near the south wall.

The tour group followed McCarter and Kalevi to the restaurant. Kalevi chatted away about the history of Suomenlinna. The SIA agent knew a fair amount about the historic site, and he made up extra details for the crowd. The tour guide tried to keep up with him, translating his commentary into English and French. She knew the history of the island and realized the guard was beginning to talk nonsense, but she figured he was nervous about the awkward situation that had disturbed the normal pattern of activities at Suomenlinna.

"If everyone will please enter the restaurant and make themselves comfortable," Kalevi announced, "Gustaf and I will check with the engineers to learn if they have finished inspecting the condition of the fortress."

Erik Valkeinen didn't like what was happening. He had visited Suomenlinna before, and the place had seemed different. The park area was deserted now, but the harsh weather explained the lack of visitors. Security personnel, except for the two men who had met the ferry, were nowhere in sight. Souvenir and gift shops were closed. There were no departing tourists, but the guard had explained the accident, Valkeinen reasoned.

Suddenly he realized what was wrong with the man's story. The towers of Suomenlinna had more than one exit. The tour group wouldn't be confined to a tower unless they had been instructed to do so to protect them.

"*Ei!*" Valkeinen cried out in warning just as several of his followers entered the restaurant along with a dozen tourists, but he was too late. The Red War

Ring members who entered the restaurant found themselves face-to-face with Yakov Katzenelenbogen and four security patrolmen armed with pistols. Katz and the guards pointed their weapons at the startled group.

*"Seis!"* a security officer ordered, clutching a Lahti pistol in both gloved hands.

The civilians gasped. Two women and a man screamed in terror, and several others raised their arms. Three of the terrorists dropped their luggage and reached inside their coats for handguns, while a fourth dove to the floor and fumbled with the drawstring of his burlap knapsack.

Katz carried his Uzi by a strap over his left shoulder, but he didn't want to use a full-auto weapon with so many innocent bystanders in the line of fire. The Israeli held the SIG-Sauer P-226 pistol ready in his left fist, the steel hooks of his prosthesis braced under the frame to steady his aim. He trained his pistol on a terrorist who had just drawn a Norwegian M-38 9 mm pistol from his coat.

The Israeli squeezed the trigger, and a hollowpoint slug smashed into the terrorist's forehead. The bullet expanded as it split bone, and the Red Ring gunman's skull burst open in a shower of blood before the horrified onlookers.

Another terrorist grabbed a small boy and prepared to use the lad for a shield or as a hostage. Katz snap-aimed his SIG-Sauer and fired two rounds. The parabellums hissed as the bullets knifed through the air inches above the boy's head. The high-velocity projectiles didn't miss their intended target. Both 9 mm slugs tore into the chest of the gunman. One bullet shattered the man's breastbone and drove him backward, but the second round plowed into his heart.

The frightened civilians responded to the shooting, some of them bolting in blind fear while others kept better self-control and dropped to the floor to avoid the line of fire. A Red Ring terrorist landed on the floor between two American tourists and yanked a Swiss Model 49 pistol from a coat pocket.

"Oh, hell," one American rasped as he pounced on the terrorist's hand and wrist to pin the gun to the floor.

"Get the bastard!" the other one declared, hammering a fist into the nape of the terrorist's neck.

The two Americans wrenched the gun from their opponent and beat him unconscious while a female Red Ring fanatic drew a compact Walther pistol. She grabbed the lady tour guide by the collar of her coat and began to raise the gun to the guide's head.

However, the lady provided a surprise. She ducked her head and turned sharply, breaking free of the female terrorist's grasp. She suddenly shoved the terrorist. Just shoved her, sending the woman staggering across the room away from the others.

The female terrorist still held the Walther pistol in her fist, and two security patrolmen opened fire with their Lahtis. A pair of 9 mm parabellums crashed into the female's chest. She dropped her weapon and slumped lifeless to the floor.

Katz turned his attention to the terrorists who had dived to the floor and extracted a Valmet M-62 from his burlap knapsack. A Finnish version of the Soviet AK-47 assault rifle, the Valmet was a deadly full-auto weapon with a folding tubular stock and a banana magazine loaded with 7.62mm cartridges.

"Drop it," Katz ordered, pointing his SIG-Sauer at the gunman.

Maybe the terrorist didn't understand Katz's words, but he clearly understood the pistol aimed at his face. The guy tossed away his Valmet rifle. It skidded across the floor as the gunman raised his hands. Katz nodded with approval and gestured with the hooks of his prosthesis to indicate that he wanted the terrorist to get to his feet.

Suddenly another Red Ring fanatic appeared at the doorway with a Danish Madsen submachine gun in his fists. The terrorist triggered his weapon, and a burst of 9 mm rounds raked the restaurant. Two bullets slammed into the chest of a security guard. At least one slug struck another guard in the upper arm. The man gasped and was spun around by the force of the bullet as the Lahti pistol fell from his trembling fingers.

A fleeing tourist was also cut down by the machine gunner. The French woman caught two 9 mm rounds between the shoulder blades. She screamed and fell forward, crashing into a table and a set of chairs and tumbling to the floor as Yakov Katzenelenbogen swung his SIG-Sauer toward the doorway.

Katz fired two rounds. One parabellum messenger tore into the side of the gunman's neck. The other struck his jawbone, smashing the mandible and shattering most of his teeth. The Madsen subgun fell from the terrorist's grasp as he collapsed across the threshold.

The man Katz had disarmed saw an opportunity and took it. He launched himself at the Israeli, planning to wrench the pistol from Katz's single hand. He was twenty years younger than the Israeli and confident that he could take Katz if he could get hold of the gun.

The terrorist didn't realize he was pitting himself against an opponent with close to forty years of combat experience. Katz dodged the younger man's attack and lashed out with the prosthesis. Steel hooks snared the Red Ring moron's right wrist and pulled him off balance. Katz quickly rammed the muzzle of his pistol under the terrorist's rib cage and drove a knee into his opponent's stomach.

The fanatic doubled up with a gasp. Katz kept the hooks of his artificial arm locked around the man's wrist as he twisted the captive limb and hammered the frame of his SIG-Sauer into the terrorist's elbow joint. Bone cracked at the elbow and wrist. The terrorist howled as his ulnar nerve seemed to ignite with fiery pain. Katz released his opponent. The Red Ring amateur clutched his shattered arm with his good hand and dropped to his knees, sobbing with pain and despair.

"Tough break," Katz said dryly as he glanced down at the vanquished foe.

OUTSIDE, THE BATTLE CONTINUED with Valkeinen and the remaining members of the Red War Ring pitted against the second attack force consisting of McCarter, James, Kalevi and more security guards. At least a dozen of the terrorists hadn't entered the restaurant. Neither had seventeen tourists who suddenly found themselves in the middle of a firefight.

Several terrorists immediately responded to Valkeinen's shouted warning by drawing their weapons. So did McCarter and Kalevi. The British ace dropped to one knee, his Browning Hi-Power held in a two-handed Weaver's grip as two Red Ring killers turned their weapons toward the two "security guards" who had escorted the group to the restaurant.

Kalevi had drawn his Lahti from shoulder leather, but the draw was clumsy because the SIA agent wasn't practiced and the front sight of his pistol had snagged on the fabric of his topcoat. The Finnish agent found himself staring into the muzzle of a terrorist's MAB pistol before he could aim his gun. Kalevi stiffened in fear, aware he was about to die.

A pistol shot erupted. Kalevi flinched from the sound and expected to feel a hot projectile rip into his flesh. Instead, the terrorist toppled backward, the French autoloader still gripped in his gloved fist. Kalevi glimpsed a scarlet spider in the center of the man's forehead when the dead terrorist landed on the snow-covered ground.

David McCarter had placed the bullet right between the man's eyes. An Olympic-class marksman, McCarter was an extraordinary pistol shot with remarkable reflexes. The Briton pivoted toward another enemy gunman who was taking aim with an old British Enfield revolver.

The Phoenix pro squeezed off a shot and pumped a Browning into the upper torso of the enemy, then immediately rolled sideways on his left shoulder as the Enfield roared. A bullet tore into the ground near the

Briton's hurtling form. McCarter landed in a kneeling position, his Browning once again trained on his opponent. The terrorist still clutched the Enfield revolver in one fist as he clamped his other hand across the bullet wound in his chest. Blood and pink froth bubbled from the man's lips as he swayed on unsteady legs.

McCarter aimed and fired. A 9 mm slug crashed into the Red Ring fanatic's skull, and the man's head jerked violently. He was done for, but more Red Ring terrorists had drawn weapons and prepared for battle.

The tourists responded to the danger in a manner identical to the civilians inside the restaurant. Some bolted in terror, while others dropped to the ground to avoid the line of fire. One terrorist had taken a Madsen chopper from a canvas bag and was aiming the Danish subgun at the backs of several fleeing tourists.

"Not today, you bastard," Calvin James whispered as he lined up the sights of his M-16 assault rifle.

The hardass from Chicago had been concealed in the museum about twenty-five yards from the restaurant. James and six security patrolmen had remained hidden from view and waited for the trap to spring. Now James and the rest of the backup unit went into action.

James squeezed the trigger of his M-16 and fired a well-controlled 3-round burst. The trio of 5.56 mm slugs smashed into the face of the terrorist who was about to gun down the helpless tourists. The killer's face seemed to disintegrate into an anonymous mask of blood, and he was dead before he could trigger the Danish blaster.

The black warrior emerged from the door of the museum and sprinted toward the restaurant. Several of the terrorists were still fumbling with bags and cases, trying to bring their weapons into play. Others had already drawn handguns or machine pistols, and two of these spotted James and swung their weapons in his direction.

A security officer stationed at a parapet walk along a flanking tower aimed his Steyr-Mannlicher rifle at the group below. He peered through the telescopic sight and centered the cross hairs on the chest of a terrorist who was about to fire an Ingram M-10 at James. The patrolman squeezed the trigger and saw the terrorist twitch as a 6.5 mm bullet smashed into his chest. The guard felt the recoil of the rifle, then lost sight of his target. He searched for the terrorist through the scope and found him sprawled in the snow.

Another enemy gunman aimed a Beretta Brigadier pistol at James, unaware he had turned his back on McCarter and Kalevi in the process. The SIA agent took advantage of that and fired his Lahti autoloader at the terrorist. Kalevi shot the Red Ringer in the middle of the spine and fired another round that bored a tunnel to the man's heart. The Italian blaster fell from the terrorist's fingers, and he wilted lifeless to the ground.

Dropping to a kneeling position, a gunsel squeezed off a shot at McCarter. A British tourist who was hugging the ground near the gunman saw the man take aim again. Bracing himself on his shoulders and upper back, the tourist lashed out a kick at the terrorist's gun. The terrorist gasped with surprise as the weapon was struck from his hand, and swiveled violently toward the tourist, hissing with anger.

A Texan who lay on the ground behind the gunman had seen the disarming of the terrorist. Not about to be outdone by an Englishman, the Texan slammed his booted foot between the terrorist's shoulder blades. The blow knocked the Red Ring flunky forward and propelled him on all fours next to the gutsy Briton. The English tourist promptly swung another kick to the gunman's face and broke his jaw.

"Nice work, feller," the Texan drawled as he glanced at the unconscious terrorist.

"Yes," the Briton replied with a nervous smile as he realized what he had done. Yet his fear was mixed with satisfaction at the outcome of their actions against the terrorist. "We did a rather good job, didn't we?"

Security guards along the flanking walls and at the museum opened fire on the terrorists' position. Most were armed with handguns or shotguns, which weren't accurate at seventy yards. However, they had been instructed by Phoenix Force to aim over the heads of the group to avoid hitting any bystanders. The men with shotguns held their fire until they could get a clear target at close range. For the moment, the guard force was only concerned with keeping the enemy off balance and convincing them to keep their heads down long enough for Calvin James to get closer and to allow McCarter and Kalevi to seek cover.

James reached a wall of the restaurant and poked his rifle barrel around the corner. A female terrorist had just unfolded the stock of a Valmet assault rifle and was preparing to open fire on the security guard shooters along the flanking walls. She didn't see Calvin James until it was too late. The black commando triggered his M-16 and blasted three 5.56 mm rounds through the female killer. Her heart burst, and she fell face first in the snow.

Calvin James retreated behind the corner an instant before a volley chewed at his shelter. Chips of stone spat from the edge of the wall, and James heard the whine of ricochets. He remained behind cover and waited for the enemy to choose another target, leaving the offensive in the hands of others.

McCarter dashed for cover at the opposite end of the building while Kalevi dropped to a kneeling stance and remained in place. The SIA agent aimed his Lahti pistol at the Valmet-toting gunman who had tried to out-ace James. However, Kalevi failed to notice Erik Valkeinen. The terrorist leader had drawn a Walther PPK from a coat pocket and fired two rounds at Kalevi. One .380 bullet missed the Finnish agent and kicked up snow near his left knee.

The second Walther round drilled into Kalevi's thigh and smashed the femur bone. The Finnish agent cried out in agony and fell sideways in the snow. Valkeinen didn't bother to pump another slug into the wounded agent. He and three fellow Red Ring terrorists were more concerned with escape than with taking out opponents.

Valkeinen and the trio of followers bolted for the east wall while two other Red Ring terrorists remained among the cluster of cowering tourists, slain gunmen and security guards at the restaurant. McCarter spotted the fleeing terrorists and aimed his

Browning Hi-Power at the nearest one. The Briton fired a well-placed 9 mm round and shot the terrorist just above the right knee. The man screamed as his leg swung out from under him. He lost his balance and tumbled to the ground, a Madsen chatter gun in his fists.

A terrorist armed with a Valmet rifle whirled and fired a hasty volley at McCarter. The Briton dropped flat on the ground, and half a dozen rounds pelted the wall of the restaurant above McCarter's prone form. He braced his feet apart, aimed the Browning and returned fire.

Two 9 mm rounds knifed under the terrorist rifleman's ribs, destroying lung tissue. The Red Ring fanatic groaned and vomited blood as he staggered backward. McCarter fired a third parabellum round and drilled the wounded gunman through the heart. The man dropped his rifle and fell lifeless, while Valkeinen and another Red Ring stooge continued to retreat from the battlefield.

The two terrorists who had remained behind didn't last long. Yakov Katzenelenbogen appeared at the doorway of the restaurant with his Uzi held ready. He triggered the submachine gun with a skilled touch and fired a neat 3-round burst into the enemy gunman, who suddenly executed an awkward shuffle, then crashed onto his back and died.

The second fanatic had removed a Heckler & Koch M-69 grenade launcher from a camera bag. The compact weapon resembled an oversize flare gun, but it fired a 40 mm explosive projectile. He raised the minicannon and pointed it at the restaurant.

Despite his wounded thigh, Kalevi sat up and aimed his Lahti pistol at the guy with the grenade launcher. The Finnish agent squeezed the trigger. A parabellum round struck the terrorist in the base of the skull. The high-velocity bullet streaked through the man's brain and punched a nasty exit hole in his forehead. He fell to the ground, the unfired M-69 still locked in his fists.

Two security patrolmen fired at Valkeinen and his last follower as the pair ran for the east tower. None of the guards were armed with rifles, and none of them were skilled pistol marksmen. Bullets ripped into the snowy ground near the terrorists' feet. As one slug tugged the sleeve of Valkeinen's topcoat, the alarmed terrorist leader yelped with fear and dropped his Walther pistol.

The other Red Ring lunatic fired a wild salvo at the guards along the flanking wall to pin them down as Valkeinen jogged to a flight of stone steps leading to the tower of the keep. The ringleader began to mount the staircase, followed by the flunky with the subgun.

A thick oak door at the base of the tower opened, and a patrolman with a shotgun emerged. He rushed to the foot of the stairs and raised his weapon. The Madsen-packing terrorist turned and swung his weapon at the guard. The shotgun roared first. Buckshot pellets blasted into the upper torso and face of the Red Ring underling. Flesh and muscle were instantly reduced to a crimson pulp, and the terrorist tumbled down the stairs in a gory heap.

Valkeinen stared down at the bloodied remnants of his companion and the black muzzle of the shotgun, which was now pointed at him. The terrorist leader

slowly raised his hands in surrender as David Mc-
Carter jogged toward the keep.

"Well, this is our lucky day," The British ace said
with a smile, gazing up at Valkeinen. "You're just the
bloke we wanted to talk to."

## 16

The body of Rolf Lautanen lay in the snow, cold and stiff. Blood had frozen against his skin and clothing like globs of hard red plastic. Rafael Encizo and Gary Manning tried to avoid looking at the slain SIA agent's mutilated body. There was nothing they could do for Lautanen now. They couldn't bury him, except to cover his corpse with snow. They couldn't even spare a strip of cloth to cover the dead man's face.

"Poor bastard," Manning muttered as he glanced at Lautanen's corpse. "Torn apart by wild animals. That's an awful way to die."

"Freezing to death isn't so great, either," Encizo commented, pulling a wolfskin pelt tightly around his shoulders and upper torso. "I think it has been colder since it stopped snowing."

"Doesn't seem so bad to me," Manning said with a yawn as he leaned against the trunk of a spruce tree. "Maybe I'm getting used to the cold...."

The Canadian's head bowed forward, and his eyes closed. Encizo grabbed Manning and shook him, making him gasp with pain as the action jarred his broken left arm.

"Damn it, Rafael!" Manning snapped, clutching his damaged arm.

"You can't go to sleep yet," Encizo insisted. "I think you might be slipping into the first stages of hypothermia."

"How about exhaustion?" Manning muttered, but he stepped away from the tree and began to walk in circles to keep his blood circulating.

"I know," Encizo said wearily. "We've been through a lot."

He glanced at the bodies of the slain wolves, which he had moved farther away from the camp area in the hope that the rest of the pack might be tempted to devour the animals rather than tangle with the men again. Encizo and Manning had also collected parts of the airplane to form the Finnish word for *help* in the snow. They hoped that a search plane would spot the sign.

Encizo and Manning had also salvaged a thick rubber tire that had probably been in the storage section of the plane. Perhaps it was part of the landing gear used for more conventional flights during warmer seasons. They placed the tire near the distress sign and filled the center with dozens of twigs. Manning still had a magnesium flare, and he hoped to use it to help signal any aircraft that might appear in the sky of endless night.

They had even found Manning's Walther P-5 pistol in the snow, but the Canadian doubted the weapon was safe to fire. The barrel had been plugged with snow, and the slide had frozen solid. The pistol would have to thaw and receive a good cleaning and oiling before Manning would use it again.

Working had been difficult due to the bitter cold and dense snowdrifts, yet they almost wished their labors weren't completed. Their tasks had broken the monotony of waiting and shivering in the dark. It had taken their minds off the howling of the wolf pack lurking somewhere in the distance. Sometimes the cries of the wolves seemed miles away. At other times the beasts sounded as if they were only inches from the two Phoenix warriors.

"Maybe we should try to walk out of here," Manning remarked. "Rescue planes might never come."

"They'll come," Encizo replied, trying to convince himself as well as Manning. "They've got to come. Somebody must have a general idea where our plane went down. Sven radioed in his position just a few minutes before the wing blew off, and they must have radar tracking stations even in Lapland. The best thing we can do is stay put."

"Yeah," Manning said in a drowsy voice. "We might have to stay put here forever...."

The roar of whirling rotor blades drew their attention toward the night sky. The sound was distant, but gradually grew louder. A tiny dot of light moved in the darkness above, a star that slowly became larger in the velvet firmament.

"Oh, God," Manning whispered, staring up at the sky, "tell me I'm not hallucinating."

"If it is, I see it and hear it, too," Encizo declared. "Use the flare, Gary. Let's not take any chances that they don't see us."

The Canadian demolitions expert removed the flare pen from his coat and placed one end between the thumb and forefinger of his left hand. His stiff fingers wouldn't clasp the pen. Manning grunted with effort, but his left hand refused to move.

"Frostbite," Manning stated tensely as he handed the pen to Encizo. "I can't do it. Just twist the pen with your hands, turning in opposite directions, and pull to break the filaments to the detonator."

Encizo followed instructions, twisting the pen and snapping the detonator filament before tossing the flare into the center of the rubber tire. The magnesium explosive erupted in a brilliant flash. The white-hot blaze ignited the twigs and branches in the center of the tire and soon began to burn the inner rim of the rubber hoop. A thick column of gray-and-black smoke rose above the sputtering flames in the middle of the tire.

"The black smoke from burning rubber could mask the fire from view in the air," Manning said grimly. "I didn't think the tire would burn this quick."

"He'll see us," Encizo said, hoping he was right.

The smoke concealed the progress of the approaching aircraft from the two men as they gazed up at the sky expectantly. They could still hear the rotor blades getting louder and louder.

Suddenly a large beam of light streaked down from the sky to illuminate the distress sign written in the snow. A forceful current of air bombarded the Phoenix pair. Gusts of snow swirled up from the ground as the artificial windstorm grew stronger. Manning and Encizo squinted as the harsh glare of a searchlight shot down on them.

"There she is!" Manning cried as he waved his good arm. "She found us!"

Encizo nodded and stared up at the helicopter. It was some sort of European version of an American Bell UH-1, with amphibious landing gear. The chop-

per descended as a sliding door to the carriage opened.
A uniformed figure leaned out the door and waved at
Encizo and Manning.

He called out in Finnish, in a voice loud enough to
be heard above the roar of the rotor blades. Then he
translated the greeting into English. "Good evening.
Do you speak English?"

The helicopter lowered to the ground, and the amphibious landing gear touched the snowy surface.
Manning and Encizo approached the chopper and
ducked their heads as they walked under the spinning
rotor blades. The man at the doors frowned when he
noticed that there were only two men.

"We were told to expect four men," he declared,
"including the pilot."

"There were four of us," Encizo replied. "But only
two of us made it."

"Get in, then," the man urged. "We'll make ar-
rangements for the bodies, but for now, we'd better get
out of here before the weather gets worse. You can tell
us what happened on the way back to Helsinki."

ERIK VALKEINEN and the other surviving members of
the Red War Ring terrorist group were taken from
Suomenlinna back to Helsinki. They were placed under arrest by the Finnish Security Intelligence Agency
and escorted to a "private clinic" at the outskirts of
the city.

Yakov Katzenelenbogen, Calvin James and David
McCarter supervised the interrogation of the prisoners. Upon request, the SIA supplied the Phoenix
Force trio with scopolamine, a powerful and poten-
tially lethal drug. Scopolamine was the most reliable

"truth serum." James was a skilled chemist, physician and former hospital corpsman. He had used scopolamine many times in the past and had never lost a patient in the process.

James didn't intend to break his record while interrogating the Red Ring terrorists. He insisted on taking as many precautions as possible to ensure the safety of each subject during an interrogation involving the use of scopolamine. James took a blood sample from each man and examined it under a microscope for evidence of blood disorders. He also used a stethoscope to check heartbeats and a sphygmomanometer to determine the blood pressure of each subject.

The Phoenix Force medic ruled out the use of scopolamine for one of the wounded terrorists who had already been given a dose of morphine. Another Red Ringer had an irregular heartbeat and appeared to have a bad liver, probably the result of drug or alcohol abuse. However, Valkeinen and the rest of his surviving followers were judged fit enough to be subjected to scopolamine injections.

Orm Karista arrived at the clinic two hours after Phoenix Force had brought the prisoners to the SIA front. James and a translator were busy questioning the subjects, who were still under the influence of the truth serum, but Katz and McCarter left the interrogation room to meet with Karista at the office of the clinic supervisor.

The SIA case officer smiled as the Phoenix pair entered the office. "You fellows did a fine job at Suomenlinna," Karista declared. "I understand the terrorists were carrying high explosives as well as automatic weapons. We would have had a real tragedy on our hands if you hadn't stopped them.''

"Could have done better," Katz replied with a sigh. "Two civilians and one security guard were killed. A few others were injured, including your man Kalevi.''

"I know," Karista assured him. "Kalevi is probably on the operating table at this moment having a bullet removed from his leg. He certainly won't die from the injury, but the doctors aren't sure he'll ever be able to walk without crutches.''

"He's a good man," McCarter stated, firing up a Player's cigarette. "Kalevi held his own with us. Bloke showed a lot of courage during that little donnybrook.''

"I'm not surprised," the SIA agent said with a nod. "I have some other good news for you. While you fellows were battling the Red Ring terrorists at Suomenlinna, the weather finally let up in Lappi. Rescue aircraft were sent out, and they located your two friends.''

"Thank God," Katz said with genuine relief. "Are they all right?''

"The big man, Jennings," Karista began. "He's in a hospital being treated for a broken arm and frostbite. If he'd been exposed to the cold for a few more hours, he probably would have lost some fingers, but the doctor in charge says he'll be fine after his arm mends. The other fellow, Sanchez or Santos or whatever name he's using, he seems to be fine. They were lucky. The pilot and Rolf Lautanen are both dead.''

"So the plane crashed?" McCarter raised his eyebrows. "They figure it was sabotage?''

"Absolutely," Karista confirmed. "Your friends saw the wing explode. Apparently it took out an engine and set fire to a fuel line. Cunning bit of sabotage. In fact, we're pretty sure we know who did it. A mechanic named Taivas had worked on the plane just before it left the airstrip. A couple of kids discovered Taivas while they were ice fishing at a lake near Vantaa."

"He's dead?" Katz inquired.

"Very dead," Karista said with a nod. "Someone chopped his head open with an ax. The corpse was apparently weighted down and dumped in the lake, but a strong undercurrent pulled it loose and it floated to the spot where the youngsters were fishing. Otherwise, the body probably wouldn't have been found until spring."

"An ax?" McCarter mused. "Different method from that used to kill the diplomats. The KGB must have arranged that style of execution to avoid being obvious."

"Although the KGB is certainly involved," Karista said, "we still don't have any proof or any idea where to find the Russians responsible."

"That was true," Katz answered. "But we've gotten some valuable information from Valkeinen and his followers. Colonel Bajanov is indeed the top control officer pulling the manipulative strings of the terrorists."

"That doesn't help much," the SIA case officer sighed. "Sanders said Bajanov disappeared, and the NSA doesn't know where he is. Does Valkeinen know where we can find the Russian?"

"Not exactly," Katz replied. "Bajanov isn't here in Helsinki, but he appears to be staying in a city or town near the capital. Another Soviet agent seems to do most of Bajanov's legwork. A man who calls himself Kharkov had been making most of the contacts with the terrorists. Valkeinen said Kharkov has also personally carried out the assassinations of the diplomats. The kidnappings and impromptu executions have been far more professional than the more indiscriminate acts of terrorism. That suggests Kharkov is a top hit man for the Kremlin's assassination section."

"Did you learn where we can locate Kharkov, or do we have two needles in the haystack instead of only one?" Karista asked, clearly frustrated by the conversation.

"Kharkov is a pro," McCarter supplied. "He doesn't make many mistakes. Amateurs make mistakes because they lack skill and experience. Professionals make mistakes when they get too bloody cocky. Assignments seem too routine after a while. The bloke gets overconfident and takes too much for granted. Kharkov has probably been assassinating people for years and never got nailed. Not only has he lost all respect for human lives, but he also probably doesn't have a very high opinion of human intelligence, either. In other words, Kharkov thinks he's smarter than everyone else."

"Did he make a mistake or didn't he?" Karista demanded.

"He made a mistake," Katz assured the SIA agent. "Not a big mistake, but big enough. Kharkov enlisted the aid of two Finnish killers named Olav and

Larrs. Apparently the pair are graduates of a waterfront protection racket. Leg breakers who have become free-lancers as hired killers."

"You see, Kharkov has been running all over Finland with those two muscle-bound Viking types," McCarter added. "Kharkov must have considered them to be his personal bodyguards and guides while operating in your country. What he failed to consider was the possibility that any of the Red Ring terrorists might recognize Olav or Larrs."

"One of Valkeinen's stooges is from the city of Kotka," Katz continued. "He remembered meeting Olav and Larrs when the pair were still working as strong-arm boys for gunrunners who've been supplying weapons to the Red Ring outfit. The terrorist flunky mentioned this to Valkeinen, who decided to check with certain underworld factions in Kotka to learn if Olav and Larrs were still residing in the city."

"Did Valkeinen learn any details about their present whereabouts?" Karista asked eagerly.

"He learned a lot of details about the pair," Katz confirmed with a smile. "Olav and Larrs have been very busy for the past few months. They've been in touch with at least one forger in Kotka, probably to purchase false ID and passports. They also hired a shoddy small-time lawyer to represent their 'confidential business interests' for a discreet arrangement with a local company with property near the waterfront. Seems the lads wanted to rent a warehouse, but they didn't want the fact known to anyone except the lawyer."

"Is Valkeinen certain of these facts?" the Finnish agent inquired.

"Absolutely," Katz stated. "Our partner, Mr. Johnson, is still supervising the interrogation and use of truth serum on the prisoners. He and some of your men are getting all the information from Valkeinen and company on tape. They're telling quite a lot, including names and addresses."

"Valkeinen must have thought he might need that information, because he went to some effort to get it," McCarter added. "Probably didn't figure he could trust the KGB and wanted an ace in the hole in case he got in trouble. Valkeinen isn't stupid. In fact, I won't be surprised if he agrees to cooperate with us even without the scopolamine. He knows the game is up as far as he's concerned."

"Kharkov underestimated Valkeinen," Katz stated. "The KGB agent assumed the leader of the Red Ring terrorists was a dim-witted fanatic like the rest of the gang. Kharkov misjudged Valkeinen's ability, just as he misjudged Olav and Larrs. Kharkov obviously thought his two henchmen would be far more careful about maintaining security. He was wrong."

"So what's our next move?" Karista asked.

"We go to Kotka and hope we can find the Russians before they abandon the site and move to another part of the country," Katz replied. "Because that's exactly what they'll do as soon as they learn what happened at Suomenlinna. They'll simply set up shop elsewhere. The KGB doesn't consist of morons. They'll figure out what went wrong and learn from their mistakes. It will be even harder to find them, and the terror and bloodshed will continue."

## 17

Lieutenant Colonel Sergei Georgeovich Bajanov adjusted the telescope mounted by the window of his office. The dawn sky was pale and laced with puffy clouds. Fishing boats moved along the chilly water. Bajanov sipped some vodka from the glass in his hand and continued to scan the Gulf of Finland until he found the small dot of land in the distance.

"Gogland Island," he said with a smile. "Home."

Bajanov didn't hear Major Kharkov enter his office. The KGB assassin quietly slipped through the half-open door and smiled as he watched Bajanov staring through the telescope like an amateur astronomer. The colonel was dressed in baggy old trousers, knee-high rubber boots and a gray turtleneck shirt. His greatcoat and wool cap were draped over the back of a chair. A well-stuffed duffel bag lay on the floor near his desk.

"Going somewhere, Comrade Colonel?" Kharkov inquired.

Bajanov gasped and dropped his glass. It shattered on the floor, and bits of glass littered the floor near his boots. Bajanov turned sharply to glare at the amused features of his fellow KGB operative. "I don't appreciate your sense of humor, Kharkov," he declared. "What are you doing here?"

"I have a radio, too, Comrade," Kharkov explained as he folded his arms across his chest. "I heard about what happened at Suomenlinna. I thought you might be packing up your things and getting ready to leave."

"Valkeinen knows about me," Bajanov stated. "If they took him alive, he'll talk. Time for me to pull out and let another case officer take over this operation."

"You don't appear to be dressed for the embassy," Kharkov remarked. "But they'll be looking for you in Helsinki, and no doubt they'll be watching the Soviet embassy with particular care."

"I'm going across the gulf to Gogland Island," Bajanov stated. "When I reach it, I'll be on Soviet territory."

"Disguised as a fisherman?" Kharkov smiled. "How droll. I assume you've considered the fact that both Finnish and Soviet vessels patrol the area."

"Of course," Bajanov replied. "Neither side will be eager to fire on a Finnish fishing vessel. I've been watching the patrol boats through my telescope for some time. The Finns don't seem too worried about anyone wishing to cross into Soviet territory. They appear to be more concerned about Soviets moving into Finnish waters. They'll probably warn me that I'm approaching Soviet waters, but I doubt the Finns will take action to stop me by force. If they do, I'll be ready for them."

"It would be ironic if you were blown out of the water by Soviet patrols instead," Kharkov remarked.

"I'll radio ahead with a password already arranged through Department Eleven in case such an emergency occurred," Bajanov replied. "Besides, that's my problem...."

Just then, Olav and Larrs appeared at the doorway, and Bajanov glared at the two Finnish hulks. They seemed to be human bookends who seemed as emotionally hollow as the Soviet killer they served. Bajanov didn't like being in the same room with the pair. They had no loyalty toward him or the cause he represented. Olav and Larrs were Kharkov's men and didn't respond to orders from anyone else.

"What are they doing here?" Bajanov demanded.

"We all heard the radio announcement together," Kharkov answered with a smile. "So we all came here together to learn what you planned to do."

"Now you know," Bajanov stated. "I'm leaving. I'm returning to the Soviet Union, and someone else will take my place in two or three months. Meantime, you and your people will have to keep a low profile and wait until Moscow contacts you."

"What about the mission, Comrade Colonel?" Kharkov asked. "The success of this operation is more important than any individual life. Yours or mine."

Bajanov stiffened. He noticed that Kharkov's right hand had slipped under the lapel of his overcoat. The assassin always carried a gun and usually carried a backup pistol, as well. Olav and Larrs were certainly armed, too. Bajanov's Makarov autoloader was in the pocket of his coat, and he would never reach it before the three killers cut him down.

"Don't be foolish, Comrade," Bajanov declared, trying to hide his fear. "My role here is over. If you kill me, you won't salvage the mission. You'll ruin any chance of resuming operations after I've had time to relay information to my superiors. The mission will have to wait a few months before it can continue, but it shall continue.''

"Perhaps,'' Kharkov said with a shrug. "But we'll have to start all over again if we wait that long. Frankly, I have strong doubts it would work. Valkeinen will tell the Finns and the Western NATO nations about the KGB involvement. Moscow will deny it, of course. Both sides will make hollow threats and accusations, but then it will blow over and things will be as they were before we started this mission.''

"Sometimes a stalemate is all one can manage,'' Bajanov commented.

"When a mission fails, it isn't a stalemate,'' Kharkov replied. "But the failure isn't my fault. I did my part in this operation. Moscow has no reason to be unhappy with me. I'm not so sure about you, Comrade.''

"I guess I'll find out when I get there,'' Bajanov stated as he reached for his coat and hat. "My boat should be waiting for me at the pier by now.''

"Then you'd better be on your way before they leave without you,'' Kharkov said as he gathered up the duffel bag. "I'll carry this for you, Colonel.''

"Thank you,'' Bajanov said with a nod. He was surprised by Kharkov's offer to help and still suspicious of the Morkrie Dela buttonman.

Kharkov cast a quizzical look at Bajanov. "We might have our differences, Comrade, but we are still fellow countrymen involved in a similar profession.''

Bajanov moved to the rear door of the office, closely followed by Kharkov with the bag. The colonel opened the door, and a strong current of icy air swept into the room. He hastily donned his coat and hat before venturing outside onto the boardwalk of the pier.

As Bajanov had predicted, a fishing vessel was waiting at the pier. It was a thirty-foot trawler with a diesel engine and a tall stovepipe that extended above the bridge. Two men stood at the bow, and another was positioned by the fishing nets at the stern. A fourth man waited on the boardwalk with his arms folded across his broad chest.

He called himself Captain Kauppias, but that was just one of many aliases he had used during his long career as a smuggler and gunrunner. Kauppias had no politics or morals. He would work for anyone and do just about anything if the price was right. He and his crew had smuggled Triad heroin into Scandinavian countries and Russian vodka into Denmark. They had helped embezzlers flee Sweden and Finland and assisted KGB operatives in infiltrating democratic nations.

Kauppias was a mercenary in the worst sense of the term. No one was quite certain what his nationality was, and it hardly mattered because he felt no loyalty toward any country or ideology. He and his men were also pirates and between contracts preyed on unsuspecting vessels in the Gulf of Finland. Kauppias was a thief, a murderer and a ruthless opportunist, yet he had never betrayed or cheated a client.

"Good morning, Captain Kauppias," Bajanov greeted as he bowed to the mercenary.

"Good morning," Kauppias returned gruffly. "We haven't got time for chitchat. If you're going with us, come now."

"Very well," Bajanov replied, taking the duffel bag from Kharkov and turning his attention to the major for the last time. "Until next time."

"Yes, yes, goodbye," Kharkov replied as he shook the colonel's hand, "and good luck."

Suddenly a voice called out from a stack of cargo crates on the pier. "Hold on, Bajanov! Your travel plans have been changed rather drastically."

Yakov Katzenelenbogen stepped from behind the crates. The Israeli held his Uzi submachine gun braced across the prosthesis of his right arm as he pointed the weapon at the men on the pier. He continued to address the group in fluent Russian.

"You can come with us and talk, or you can stay here and die," Katz explained calmly. "Make your choice."

Bajanov was too startled to respond. The colonel had been deskbound too long to remember how to deal with such situations. Kharkov immediately leaped to the cover of the doorway of Bajanov's office while Captain Kauppias cursed under his breath and threw himself to the boardwalk. The smuggler sprawled on his belly and pulled an old WWII German P.08 Luger pistol from a coat pocket.

The crew of Kauppias's vessel was tough, and they always expected trouble. One man at the bow scooped up a Valmet automatic rifle while another grabbed a Czech-made Skorpion machine pistol. Neither of them realized that three assault rifles were already trained on the fishing boat.

Calvin James was stationed on the deck of a garbage scow less than a hundred yards from the trawler. He used the corner of the bridge for a post rest as he aimed his M-16 and triggered a 3-round burst into the chest of the pirate with the Valmet. The thug screamed, and as he fell backward his head smashed through a window of the pilothouse.

An SIA marksman who was positioned at the end of the pier opened fire with an FAL rifle equipped with a Bushnell scope at the same instant James triggered another M-16 burst. Three 5.56 mm rounds and one 7.62 mm bullet slammed into the upper body of the Skorpion-toting goon. The impact spun the man around, and he toppled over the handguard to splash into the frigid water below.

Katz didn't even glance up at the crew on the boat. He had supreme faith in his men and realized that James would take care of any threat from the vessel—with the assistance of the backup team supplied by Orm Karista. The Phoenix Force commander concentrated on the three men at the pier. Kharkov had ducked into the building, Bajanov seemed as frozen as an arctic snowman, and Kauppias had adopted a prone position and drawn a weapon. Katz had no trouble choosing his target.

The Uzi snarled and ripped a trio of slugs into the head and shoulders of the crooked captain. The Luger slipped from Kauppias's gloved fingers as his skull burst open in a spray of blood.

The pirate at the stern of the trawler ducked under the handguard and reached beneath the nets to seize a Soviet-made RPD light machine gun and a box of F-1 hand grenades. He uncovered the weapons and was preparing to aim the Russian chattergun in the general direction of Katz and the riflemen. When he was spotted by a second SIA sniper posted at the opposite end of the pier. Karista's man waited for the back of the smuggler's head to appear in the cross hairs of the scope mounted on his Valmet rifle.

The agent squeezed the trigger. Three projectiles split bone and tore off the top of the pirate's skull. The man dropped his weapons and collapsed across the fishing nets, his life switched off in the flicker of an instant.

Colonel Bajanov raised his hands. He considered reaching for the Makarov pistol in his pocket, but realized it would be a futile gesture and would only get him killed. Suicide had never appealed to Bajanov, and it didn't seem any more attractive while he stared into the muzzle of Katz's Uzi.

MAJOR KHARKOV KICKED the door shut and dashed to the cover of the desk in Bajanov's office. He hastily drew a Model 38 autoloader from shoulder leather. The pistol was a Norwegian version of the Walther P1. He had used the gun to assassinate several targets since he arrived in Finland, but he had never fired the M-38 at opponents who could shoot back.

"What's happening?" Olav demanded. The big redhead and his blond clone had heard the shooting and had already ducked for cover behind the desk before Kharkov charged into the office.

"It's an ambush, you moron," Kharkov snapped. "What did you think it was? Fireworks in honor of Bajanov's departure?"

"We've got to get out of here," Larrs rasped, drawing a Lahti pistol.

"The truck is parked out front," Olav declared, working the slide to his own Lahti to chamber a round.

"So are the enemy," Kharkov remarked with a twisted smile. "They've certainly got the building surrounded, and they'll have all the exits covered. We're trapped, gentlemen."

"We'll make a run for the truck," Olav insisted. "That is still our best chance."

"Yes," Larrs agreed. "Even if we have to fight our way to the vehicle, that is better than staying here."

"You'll never make it," Kharkov stated, apparently amused by the situation. He reached inside his coat for his backup pistol, a WWII vintage Hungarian Model 37. "Better to stay here and let them come to us. Then we can take a few of them with us when we die."

"You're insane," Olav hissed through clenched teeth.

"Maybe I am," the Soviet assassin admitted, holding the M-38 in one fist and the Model 37 in the other. "But I know death better than anyone. I've delivered it many times in the past, and now the time has come for me to receive it. I really don't mind as long as I get to die the way I've always hoped to. Gloriously." Kharkov chuckled as if he was planning a nasty practical joke rather than discussing his own death.

But Olav and Larrs had heard enough. They decided the Russian was crazy, and they didn't share his death wish. The pair bolted from the desk and headed for the door that led to the storage section of the warehouse.

The Finnish killers entered the bay area. Columns of wooden crates surrounded the pair. They glanced up at the catwalk above the boxes, half expecting to see enemy gunmen stationed there. Nothing stirred above them. Relieved, Olav and Larrs stealthily headed for the front exit.

"Freeze, you furry buggers!" David McCarter ordered as he poked the stubby snout of his M-10 Ingram around the corner of a crate he was using for cover.

"Drop the guns!" Rafael Encizo added as he appeared from behind another crate with his H&K MP-5 machine pistol pointed at the pair. "I'm in a lousy mood, so don't fool around with me today!"

Encizo had left the hospital in Helsinki where Gary Manning remained with a fresh cast on his broken arm. The Cuban had slept for four hours and then insisted the SIA take him to Karista so he could join his teammates. He had assured the others that he was fit for duty and had found out that Phoenix Force planned to check out the warehouse in Kotka.

The commandos had discovered that Colonel Bajanov was inside the building and that Kharkov had arrived with Olav and Larrs. Phoenix Force and the SIA quickly arranged an ambush and waited to spring their trap. While Katz, James and the snipers covered the rear, McCarter and Encizo had entered through the front of the warehouse. They had the real leaders of the terrorist activity in Finland boxed inside the building and didn't intend to let any of them get away this time.

Neither Olav nor Larrs understood English, but the meaning of the weapons pointed in their direction needed no translation. The Finns dropped their guns and raised their hands. McCarter scraped his boot along the floor in an exaggerated forward motion. He repeated the action and nodded at the pair. Olav and Larrs understood the crude charade-style message and kicked their Lahti pistols across the floor toward McCarter and Encizo.

"That's good," the Briton remarked. "You blokes keep this up, and we'll get you some new flea collars before they throw your arse in prison."

"Better than they deserve," Encizo added.

Kharkov peered out the doorway of the office and saw that Olav and Larrs had been caught off guard by two opponents in the bay area. The assassin aimed his pistols around the edge of the doorway and tried to point each gun at a Phoenix pro.

"Hell!" McCarter shouted as he ducked behind a crate.

Encizo followed his example. A slug from the Hungarian pistol chipped wood from the corner of the box that served him as cover. The Cuban immediately returned fire with his MP-5. The Heckler & Koch blast machine ripped a trio of holes in the wall near Kharkov's position. The Soviet killer managed to avoid getting tagged by Encizo's volley and retreated back into the office.

Olav and Larrs took advantage of the distraction and dashed for shelter behind separate columns of crates. Kharkov peeked around the edge of the doorway and retreated as McCarter triggered a burst of

Ingram rounds. Parabellums chewed the door frame but missed their target.

"Sneaky bastard," McCarter growled as smoke rose from the muzzle of his M-10. "Show yourself again."

Suddenly the crates the Briton was using for cover tumbled toward him like a wooden avalanche. He couldn't dodge the boxes without presenting himself as a target for Kharkov. He ducked and covered his head as best he could as the heavy crates crashed down on him.

A box struck the Ingram from his grasp, and another knocked him to the floor. Dazed, the Briton gazed up to see Olav grinning down at him. The big redhead had pushed the crates over and attained the desired result. Olav's scarlet beard parted to display two rows of white teeth as he held a fire ax in both fists and stepped forward.

Encizo saw his partner in trouble and tried to aim his MP-5 at Olav when a battle scream erupted behind him. He turned to see Larrs leap forward with the scramasax in his fist. The blond hulk had crept along the wall to Encizo's position and waited for a chance to attack with the big Viking knife.

The Cuban raised his H&K machine pistol, but he was too late. Larrs slammed into him, and both men fell to the floor. Encizo landed on his back with Larrs on top. Larger, heavier and more than a decade younger than Encizo, Larrs pinned the Phoenix fighter to the floor and wrenched the MP-5 from his fingers. The gun skidded across the floor as Larrs raised the twelve-inch blade and prepared to drive the steel point into Encizo's neck.

Sliding forward, Encizo slithered under his opponent. The blade of the scramasax narrowly missed delivering serious injury to the Cuban's head as the sharp edge parted Encizo's raven-black hair and cut the scalp at the top of his skull. His strength increased by fear, Encizo shoved at Larrs's left thigh with both hands and threw the man off balance.

Larrs fell sideways as Encizo rolled away and scrambled to his feet. He drew his Cold Steel Tanto as Larrs rose and adopted a knife-fighter's stance. Encizo glanced down at the scramasax. He had seen machetes smaller than his opponent's Viking knife. The blade was twice the size of Encizo's six-inch Tanto. Larrs smiled, waved the scramasax slightly and attacked.

Encizo dodged a lunge and slashed with the Tanto at Larrs's wrist above the scramasax. Larrs turned his wrist and parried the knife attack with the blade of his knife. Steel rang against steel, and Larrs executed a fast sweeping cut to Encizo's belly. The Cuban's thick parka saved him from injury, but the deep cut in the cloth warned him that the next stroke could be fatal.

The Finnish killer executed a short stab at Encizo's face. The Cuban raised his blade and weaved backward to avoid the attack, but the tactic was just a feint. Larrs lashed out with a boot aimed at Encizo's groin, but struck the Cuban's thigh muscle. The blow staggered Encizo and knocked him into a wall. Larrs hissed and lunged, his scramasax poised for Encizo's heart.

The Phoenix pro sidestepped the knife thrust and hooked an overhand stroke with the Tanto. His arm crossed above Larrs's knife-wielding arm as he stepped

forward to drive the point of the Tanto into his opponent's chest. Larrs shrieked as the sharp steel bit
deep into his solar plexus.

Encizo released the knife and left the Tanto lodged
in his opponent. He swiftly grabbed Larrs's elbow and
shoved against his shoulder, slamming the man into
the wall face first. The impact drove the Tanto deeper,
and the killer's screams ended abruptly. He fell to the
floor with the handle of the Tanto jutting from his
chest. All six inches of the blade were buried in his
lifeless flesh.

Kharkov saw the struggle between Encizo and
Larrs. McCarter and Olav were also locked in hand-to-
hand combat. The Briton had managed to dodge
Olav's ax swings, but he couldn't draw his Browning
pistol without giving Olav a chance to chop his arm
off. McCarter needed more room to clear his weapon,
and Olav didn't intend to oblige him. Kharkov held his
fire, unsure which opponent to fire on until he saw
Encizo take out Larrs.

The Soviet assassin prepared to aim his pistols at the
Cuban, but the sound of movement within the office
drew his attention. An SIA agent had kicked open the
exit door and entered from the pier, a Valmet rifle held
in his fists. Kharkov promptly turned and fired his M-
38 pistol before the agent could bring his Valmet into
use.

A 9 mm round caught the SIA man in the stomach.
He cried out, and as he started to double up, Kharkov's Model 37 barked twice. Two more bullets
smashed into the agent. The man had just collapsed on
the floor when Katzenelenbogen suddenly appeared
and sprayed the office with a salvo of Uzi rounds.

Kharkov dove across the threshold of the lead door and scurried into the bay area to avoid the Israeli's deadly attack. The Russian bolted toward a flight of wooden stairs that led to the catwalk above the bay section. He pounded up the stairs, firing his Model 37 at the office doorway to discourage anyone from following him.

Olav raised his ax to attempt another swing at McCarter. The Briton suddenly stepped forward and grabbed the ax handle with both hands. Olav instinctively pulled the ax back to try to retain possession of the weapon. McCarter moved with the tugging motion and snapped his head forward to smash the front of his skull into the bridge of his opponent's nose.

McCarter delivered another head butt and struck Olav twice in the same spot. Cartilage cracked, and blood oozed from the big Finn's nostrils. Olav bellowed with rage and shoved the ax handle to push McCarter away. The British warrior didn't resist. He bent his knees and fell backward, breaking his fall with his rump and left thigh. His right foot rose to meet Olav's belly as he pulled the Finn forward and rolled onto his back.

The Briton straightened his right knee and hauled Olav head over heels in a judo circle throw. He released the ax handle and allowed the Finn to sail overhead and crash to the floor. McCarter jumped to his feet and yanked the Browning from leather as Olav staggered upright and raised the ax.

McCarter snap-aimed and opened fire. A slug punched into Olav's chest. The Finn grunted and charged forward, the ax still clutched in his fists. McCarter pumped another Browning slug through the big man's heart, but Olav kept coming. Blood drooled from the Finn's open mouth, and his eyes were filled with pain and fury as he raised the ax over his head and prepared to strike.

David McCarter fired a third round and blasted a bullet hole in the center of his opponent's forehead. The ax slipped from lifeless fingers and clattered to the floor. Olav fell forward. McCarter stepped aside as the dead Finn crashed to the floor.

A bullet hissed an inch from McCarter's shoulder, making the Briton utter a clipped obscenity and dive to the floor. Another shot snarled from the catwalk above the bay. The bullet tore into the wall above McCarter's position.

Rafael Encizo saw the muzzle flash of Kharkov's M-38 pistol as the Soviet assassin leaned over the wooden handrail of the catwalk to fire at the British commando. Encizo raised his H&K and fired two rounds at Kharkov's position.

One bullet sizzled harmlessly past the Russian's ear, but the other parabellum caught Kharkov in the right shoulder. The hot projectile tore past flesh and muscle to shatter bone. The Norwegian pistol dropped from Kharkov's fingers as the force of the high-velocity slug spun him around. He fell against the long-neglected and half-rotted handrail. Wood cracked and crumbled under the Russian's weight.

Kharkov screamed as the handrail gave way. He toppled from the catwalk and plunged ten feet to smash into a crate. The small of his spine struck the corner of the heavy box. The lumbar vertebrae crunched, and Kharkov's screams ended abruptly as his body dropped limply to the floor. The Russian's back was broken.

"Is everybody all right?" Yakov Katzenelenbogen asked, stepping from the office doorway with the Uzi canted across his shoulder.

"If you don't count the bad guys," Encizo replied, returning his H&K pistol to the holster under his left arm. "How did everything go outside?"

"We managed to take Bajanov alive," Katz explained. "One of Karista's people was killed, but no other casualties on our side. Bajanov is our only prisoner. Of course, he was the big fish we were after."

"That means the KGB plot just had its plug pulled," McCarter said cheerfully. "Ought to be pretty embarrassing for the Kremlin."

"Private embarrassment," Katz replied with a shrug. "Nobody wants an international stink over this. Finland needs to continue neutral relations with the Soviets. Moscow certainly won't want this matter to be public, and Washington will be happy to resume business as usual. My guess is everyone will agree to blame the whole mess on the Red War Ring terrorists. A bunch of Marxist fanatics who were trying to stir up trouble for Finland and the West. The KGB connection will never be official. Moot point, since the violence is over and people will be relatively safe in Finland now—including diplomats from America."

"Let's go to the hospital and tell Gary what he missed here," McCarter said with a sly grin. "Poor chap missed most of the action this time."

"You weren't with us in Lapland," Encizo said dryly. He stopped to gather up his MP-5 machine pistol as he added, "I don't care where we go right now, as long as it's someplace warm."

# Available soon!
# SuperBolan #11

# ANVIL OF HELL

Bolan tracks nuclear fuel across the stony wastes of the Sudanese Sahara to thwart the plans of a powerful consortium to attack the Middle East.

GOLD
EAGLE

SB-1

**A secret arms deal
with Iran ignites a powder keg,
and a most daring mission is
about to begin.**

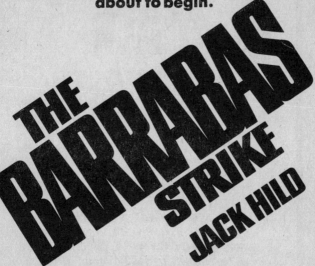

Nile Barrabas and his soldiers undertake a
hazardous assignment when a powerful top-
secret weapon disappears and shows up in
Iran.

# Take
# 4 explosive books
# plus a
# mystery bonus
# FREE

Mail to **Gold Eagle Reader Service**®

In the U.S.
P.O. Box 1394
Buffalo, N.Y. 14240-1394

In Canada
P.O. Box 609
Fort Erie, Ont.  L2A 5X3

**YEAH!**   Rush me 4 free Gold Eagle novels and my free mystery
bonus. Then send me 6 brand-new novels every other month as
they come off the presses. Bill me at the low price of just $14.95'—
an 11% saving off the retail price - plus 95¢ postage and handling
per shipment. There is no minimum number of books I must buy. I
can always return a shipment and cancel at any time. Even if I never
buy another book from Gold Eagle, the 4 free novels and the
mystery bonus are mine to keep forever.          166 BPM BP7F

_____

Name                      (PLEASE PRINT)

_____

Address                                       Apt. No.

_____

City                    State/Prov.         Zip/Postal Code

_____

Signature (If under 18, parent or guardian must sign)

This offer is limited to one order per household and not valid to
present subscribers. Price is subject to change.

                                    4E-SUB-1D